MW01109710

To Marry a Morgan

Morgan

(Book One in The Pathways to Romance Series)

By

Cinnamon Worth

To Marry a Morgan copyright 2019 by Cinnamon Worth. All Rights Reserved.

All rights reserved. No part of this book may be reproduced in any form or by any electronic or mechanical means including information storage and retrieval systems, without permission in written form from the author. The only exception is by a reviewer, who may quote short excerpts in a review.
Cover Design by Blue Water Books

This book is a work of fiction. Names, characters, places, and incidents either are the product of the author's imagination or are used fictitiously. Any resemblances to actual persons, living or dead, events, or locales is entirely coincidental.

Cinnamon Worth

First Print: May 2019

Your value doesn't decrease based on someone's inability to see your worth.
Cinnamon Worth

Dedicated to my wonderful readers. Thank you for all your support and feedback.

Table of Contents

Chapter One

Phillip Heartford walked into the main hall of his gentleman's club and scanned the dining room. Considering the exclusivity of the club, there was a surprising number of patrons. The heavenly scent of fried bacon and roasted veal filled the room, revealing the reason for the crowd. White soup was on today's menu. His attention drifted toward the table he almost regarded as a second home. His eyes lit in delight, and he sent his friend Fitz Atherton a dazzling smile. He was rewarded with a wave, inviting him forward.

"Heartford," Fitz greeted before refilling his glass. "I've heard a rumor you are about to inherit the family estate."

Phillip, who had not anticipated that such news had already become public knowledge, was caught off guard by this greeting. A grimace pierced his carefully constructed façade. Fortunately, Fitz, being engaged in pouring his drink, had not noticed the slip.

Looking up from his task, Fitz gave Phillip a quizzical look. Pointing to a black bundle in Phillip's hands, he said, "It appears you forgot to check your coat."

Settling into his chair, Phillip shrugged, as if it was very common to bring his coat to the table. "I suppose, I did," he said. He placed his balled-up coat on his lap. "Do you think I could order a cup of milk?"

Fitz looked at him as though he had lost his mind. Picking up a decanter, he looked at the amber colored liquid tenderly. "Do you have any idea how well-aged this bourbon is? It is a masterpiece."

"Then I shall take a glass of that as well."

"I do not believe bourbon and milk go well together," Fitz explained. His eyes flicked over to Phillip's lap. He leaned over and said, "I don't mean to alarm you, Heartford, but your coat is moving."

A quick glance around the room revealed the other patrons were all absorbed in their own conversations, and the one staff member on the floor was busy piling dirty dishes on a large tray. Phillip pulled back the edge of his coat, revealing a sleeping kitten. "She's a stray."

"Well, put the coat and its contents on the floor between us. It will be less noticeable."

Gently, Phillip lowered his coat, careful to keep from disturbing the feline's sleep.

Nearly as soon as he had straightened back up, he noticed Caleb James approaching. Caleb moved with such grace, he practically glided across the room. On more than one occasion, Phillip had been caught off guard by his stealthy approach. He immediately stood and again produced a radiant smile. "Caleb! What a nice surprise." With a wave of his hand, he motioned for Mr. James to join them, then he walked to a nearby buffet, giving Caleb a friendly pat on the arm as he passed. When he returned, he was carrying a third glass. Caleb remained standing, so Phillip pulled out a chair. "Have a seat," he said to ensure there was no confusion.

"Heartford, you are so hospitable, you will be eaten alive once your career takes off," Fitz said in an amused tone.

"It costs nothing to be nice." Noting that Caleb remained standing still, Phillip added, "It's Bourbon—and well-aged."

Caleb looked down at the chair. A flicker of regret passed over his features. "Not today, I am afraid. I've just stopped by to find you both."

"Come," Fitz said in a persuasive and inviting tone. "If Caleb James, is actively seeking out someone other than Miss Walker, it must be important. We must hear more. And our friend here," he clasped Phillip on the shoulder, "is just about to take over the family estate. I am sure we can find some fun in scaring him about all of his pending responsibilities."

"While I delight in torturing Phillip, I am actually on a mission to deliver these." Caleb reached into his inner breast pocket and retrieved two items. He handed one to each of the gentlemen. The folded papers gave no hint of the contents, but the seal pushed into the wax could only mean these were invitations to the Everlys' annual garden party. "I hope you can make it," he said. Phillip knew this had been said only as a formality. It was a foregone conclusion that anyone receiving such an invitation would be in attendance.

Although the Everlys' annual garden party took place in Kent, the event had always been the toast of the town. Everybody who was anybody would leave the bustling city of London in the middle of the season, should they be lucky enough to secure an invitation, that was. The distance to the Everlys' estate meant a week away from London at the height of the season. But considering the pedigree of those on the guest list and the splendor of the grounds, such minor inconveniences were inconsequential. Still, over the years there had been guests who, due to either ignorance or arrogance, felt compelled to suggest to Mrs. Everly that she consider hosting the event in the summer. Mrs. Everly would smile and thank them for their suggestions. The following year, the names of these individuals would be struck from the guest list. For it was perfectly clear that it was the graceful butterflies that fluttered about, the intoxicating scent of flowers, the brilliant bursts of colors from the buds and blooms, and the promise of new love which always accompanied spring, that made her event what it was.

Fitz lifted his invitation like it was made of gold and carefully secured it in his pocket. Phillip dropped his on the table.

"You can't be spared for even a single drink?" Phillip asked holding up the tumbler with one hand and clasping the decanter with the other.

"I'm afraid not." Caleb turned to go then paused. He took a few steps toward Phillip. "Is that a cat at your feet?" he asked looking down at a small ball of fur curled up next to a chair.

"He found a stray on his way here and snuck it into the club under his coat," Fitz explained.

Phillip looked at Fitz. "You make it sound as if I intend to leave it here," he said. "I will drop it off at home, but I didn't want to keep you waiting."

Caleb snickered. "Don't get caught. The fine is enormous." He raised an eyebrow, pointed to the unopened invitation sitting in front of Phillip, and asked, "You will be going, won't you? I'd nearly forgotten your disregard for following the obvious path." It was a cross between a demand and a question.

"I will think about it," Phillip said before releasing the cup intended for Caleb and refilling his own.

Caleb shook his head in apparent disbelief. "If you do not attend this year, I cannot ensure I will be able to continue to convince my aunt to invite you."

"Will it help if I send flowers to apologize?" Phillip asked as he placed the stopper in the decanter.

"It will help if you make an appearance," Caleb snapped before taking his leave.

Fitz leaned back in his chair and stretched out his legs. His face scrunched up as he studied Phillip. "What was that about?" he asked.

"Humm?" Phillip asked, clearly confused.

"How could you decline an invitation? And why would you need to think about attending?" Fitz took a sip of his beverage. "I agree that the party itself is the very essence of boredom, but with your political aspirations, you know as well as I do that you cannot pass on such an opportunity." His voice dropped. "You can always do as I do and use the days leading up to the party to meet who you need to meet and charm who you need to charm, before running to the hills to avoid the invasion of the mercenaries."

"It is not the party itself I have been avoiding," Phillip said quietly. "Marymoor is but five miles from Brighton Manor."

Fitz set down his glass and leaned in toward Phillip. "Your home? Why, that should be even more reason to visit." Fitz shook his head. "I cannot imagine the state it must be in. And, if you are to inherit soon, you will want to get started right away on getting it in order." He took a sip before continuing, "When was the last time you visited?"

"Five years ago," Phillip said. He stared into the fire, marshaling his features to present a blank slate.

"Oh." The word was said in the same manner that may have been used had Fitz just walked into a store being burglarized. And just as he would under this hypothetical scenario, Fitz slowly retreated.

Fitz, however, did not possess the grace inherent in Caleb. His movement caught Phillip's attention. Phillip turned from the fire, replacing the distant, forlorn look he had been wearing with the friendly, relaxed expression he had donned prior to mentioning Marymoor. "But you are right about the mercenaries. I have heard some stories about the lengths they go to in order to secure a loveless marriage. Perhaps I should go. I could watch and learn a lesson or two."

"It does not work, my friend. Even if you know all their tricks, they will still try to snare you."

"I do not mean to avoid them," Phillip explained. "I hope to join them."

"You? A mercenary? Impossible," Fitz proclaimed. "If your family was having financial difficulties, I would have heard about it." Fitz's father was indeed a powerful man. Half the debts held in the city were owed to the Duke of Hastingridge.

Phillip waved his hand as if to brush away such a ridiculous notion. "Oh, no. We have no issues on that front." He took a sip of his drink. "Besides, if I sell myself, it will not be for money."

Stroking his chin, Fitz asked, "You are in want of a woman from a noble family then? I did not think you the sort."

Phillip shook his head. "No. I already have sufficient access to those I wish to be acquainted with. I do not care about my wife's lineage."

"You have connections and are not in need of money so, what are you up to?"

"I have been putting off the repayment of a favor," Phillip explained. His mask slipped ever so slightly. Despite his best effort, a bit of emotion choked his voice "But the time has come for me to marry, so I suppose I must return. It is time I repay my debt."

Fitz shook his head. "It is bad enough you are being forced to relinquish your freedom."

Silence fell over the table, both men absorbed in their own thoughts. Fitz's foot began to tap, and Phillip's steady gaze never left the flames within the fireplace.

After a moment, Fitz's hand smacked the table, drawing Phillip's attention. "I know a surprising number of eligible bachelors who can take your place and would be pleased to repay me with such a simple favor. Let me talk to the man you owe."

"You cannot," Phillip replied. "My brother is dead." He looked into his glass and released a sigh. "I cannot bring him back, but I can live the life he should have had."

"Your brother was engaged?" Fitz asked.

A bitter laugh escaped Phillip's lips. "No, he was not. But I do not intend to marry the woman he would have asked. Julia belongs to him, and had he lived, she would likely be my sister. I am not so dishonorable to attempt to rob him of her love, but..." He closed his eyes and his shoulders slumped. "Johnathan would have wanted me to do all that is in my power to protect her, and that would be more easily accomplished if I married her sister."

Fitz mulled over this idea. "Is she attractive?" he asked.

"The sister?"

Phillip offered a nod. "The last time I saw her she had the face of an angel."

"Well then, it cannot be too terrible."

Phillip had to bite his tongue to avoid saying anything further that could damage the reputation of his future wife.

Chapter Two

"Allison, thank goodness I've found you." Though no more than a few yards separated them, Julia hurried up the remaining steps. Her heart raced and she was anxious to be within arm's reach of her sister. She knew she was being silly. Just because Allison had been difficult to locate, did not mean she would simply disappear now that she'd been found.

Without a word, Allison turned. She stood, holding her teacup in one hand and saucer in the other. She brought the liquid to her lips and took a sip. Her large, blue eyes remained visible over the rim of the cup as she stared at Julia.

"I have been wandering around for nearly twenty minutes looking for you. Where have you been, and are you unwell?"

Tilting the cup upright, Allison's perfect red lips formed a smirk. "I am fine. I have been here. Why would you worry?"

"It was just that I hadn't seen you, and one never knows," Julia mumbled. She felt foolish for voicing her concerns out loud. Allison was certainly not in any danger, but she had been known to sulk. Even though Julia was the younger of the two, she felt extremely protective and maternal toward Allison. "I know no one here," Julia continued, hoping to change the subject. As her anxiety dissipated, her fatigue made itself known. Her shoulders fell, and she could hear her mother reminding her to stop slouching. She felt her stomach's silent rumbling. "How are we a mere three miles from our home, yet completely surrounded by strangers?"

"I had thought that was the draw of the Everlys' parties," Allison said. She carefully set her cup back onto its dainty saucer.

"Perhaps." Julia turned slightly, looking over her shoulder and surveying the crowd. "Under the right circumstances, I would agree. But if you are in a room filled with strangers, without a soul to introduce you, what is the point?"

The pair stood on the terrace that overlooked the gardens. The grounds, which had been designed by the famed landscape artist Andre La Norre, could have rivaled any in Europe. Dozens of people stood at the railings, which offered the best views of this masterpiece. Between the perfectly sculpted topiaries, stood handsomely attired men and women playing games, partaking in refreshments, or quietly chatting. The scent of jasmine, gardenias, and roses filled the air, and the clear blue sky provided the guests with ample sunlight.

Allison replied dryly, "We are not in a room."

"Well, no, but the concept remains the same," Julia said. A hint of annoyance crept into her tone, and she inwardly cringed in dismay. Her gaze shifted as she faced her sister head on. Behind Allison, several yards in the distance, stood a table covered in a cream-colored linen edged in lace. Silver platters and tiered trays crowded the surface. Each platter held a new delight, cakes in every variety, biscuits drizzled with chocolate and cream, strawberries, and bonbons. Julia's expression shifted into one of longing.

Allison glanced over her shoulder before her eyes refocused a narrowed glare onto Julia. "Do not even think about it," she snapped. "You know what Father would say."

Rolling her eyes, Julia mumbled, "A gentleman might overlook the color of a lady's hair if it is set in a lovely coiffure, and the imperfections of one's complexion might go unnoticed behind the right shades of fabric, but no seamstress can hide the figure a woman carries."

"That is correct. Now, those treats may look tempting, but they cannot be worth the risk of becoming an old maid."

"No, I suppose not." Julia's voice betrayed her conflicted feelings on this point. *If only that was all one needed to do to avoid such a fate. And since I am destined to die alone, why can't I enjoy just one dessert?* Julia could not count the number of bibs she had embroidered while listening to her mother's friends discussing the latest adorable baby to join their small community. To hear them speak, one would think all babies were attractive. Julia knew that the midwives would not agree. Some children were simply born to be...different, and she was one of them. But all good stories required a fair maiden and a deformed witch, and she was the perfect person to play opposite Allison. With her golden hair and devastatingly spectacular eyes, Allison needed no help in assuming her role as the heroine. But it was her slender frame Julia most envied. A sigh slipped out. Her sister would never understand the challenges she faced in such matters, for it was clear that Allison was incapable of becoming plump. "I do not even know why father continues save his musings. They are never pithy or entertaining," she added.

"It is true. He is no Richard Saunders," her sister conceded. Allison eyed the empty cup in her hand, and the two turned and walked in tandem toward a smaller table, cluttered with dirty dishes. Once they arrived, Allison added her saucer to the little pile of similar plates. Next to this pile sat a stack of four teacups, nested carefully to create a teetering tower. With a steady hand, Allison balanced her cup on the top. It was a testimony to her grace that she'd not only successfully set her cup in place, but she had made it look so effortless.

Julia quickly walked away and beckoned her sister to follow. Even *looking* at the leaning tower made her nervous. She was certain she would exhale or make some sudden movement in the general proximity of the table and manage to generate enough wind to tip the scales—sending all of the poor little cups to their doom.

"Julia," Allison called while lengthening her stride. If she was attempting to catch up, her efforts were futile. Her breath short, she called, "Do you think me a horse? Slow your pace!"

Once she was far enough away from the table of dishes that she knew she could not be held responsible should anything go amiss, Julia stopped.

Joining her, Allison put her hands on her waist, and bent forward greedily gulping air. After a few moments, she straightened and said, "Goodness. At that speed I nearly thought you had seen Uncle Edward."

"I am sorry," Julia said as she reached out and placed her hand on her sister's sleeve. "I did not mean to tire you." Her eyes drifted back to the table laden with food. *Am I imagining feeling lightheaded?* "If the seamstress has run out of all the fabric that might help with a girl's complexion, do you think there would be any harm in feeding her?"

Allison straightened herself. "Tell me that you are not still thinking you are going to crawl away and live in some hovel...alone."

"I never said hovel," Julia protested. "And it is not that I do not wish to marry—should the right man ask. It is just that I am practical, and you must admit, I have turned no heads at all so far."

"We leave for London on Friday. There, you will have no dearth of suitors. I assure you."

Julia's eyes grew wide as she focused on a distant point

over Allison's shoulder. Allison turned and moaned. A well-dressed man in his middle years was waving to them as he walked toward the terrace.

"Humm." Allison turned back to face Julia. She smiled wryly. "You were hoping to locate someone who could provide introductions. And with our uncle's connections, you might find a suitor sooner than I thought."

A chill ran down Julia's spine. She reached over and grabbed her sister's arms. "Allison," she said as she squeezed her hands, "I implore you. Do not send me off with Uncle Edward."

Allison cocked her head to the side and smirked. "He knows everyone here, and he is really not so bad."

"Normally no," Julia agreed, "But we both know why he comes to Brighton Manor. It is so he can regale anyone who will listen with the tale of his bravery in rescuing that woman. I have heard the story more times than I can count. I believe I will go insane if I must endure hearing it one more time."

"How uncharitable of you," Allison chastised. "How can you begrudge our kind and lonely uncle for wishing to share tales of his youth?"

Before she could respond, the booming voice of her uncle called, "Allison! Julia!"

Julia forced herself to smile. She then looked to Allison and noted an expression she thought probably mirrored her own. "Well, if it isn't my two favorite nieces," Uncle Edward greeted. He chuckled and tipped his hat. "Lovely party, isn't it? I was just reminiscing how today is so very much like a day many years ago..."

When he stopped speaking rather abruptly, the sisters looked at each other, searching for answers to explain this sudden change.

"Mr. Morgan?"

Julia turned her head and there, standing a foot behind her, was a young man. He looked vaguely familiar, but had they previously met, she was certain she would have remembered.

"I do apologize for interrupting, but when I saw you, I just couldn't stop myself," the gentleman said. His face appeared to radiate with admiration. "You are a legend. Why, wasn't it here, on these very grounds, where you rescued a young woman?"

Uncle Edward's chest swelled, and his lips settled into a self-satisfied grin, "How very extraordinary. I was just about to tell my nieces that very tale."

The young man's mouth fell open. "Surely, they must already know of the extraordinary bravery and daring you showed. I was not even born when the event occurred, yet I first heard of it two towns over."

"Yes," Julia added quickly, "I do remember the story. Very vividly, in fact."

"Ah." Edward nodded and turned toward Allison.

She was staring intently at the young gentleman and was so startled when her name was spoken a moment later, she practically jumped.

"Allison," Edward said, calling her out of her daydream, "the last time we were here, I recall showing Julia the location where the incident took place. At the time, you had a headache and were not able to join us. Would you like me to show it to you now?"

Allison's eyes flickered up at the younger man. Julia was certain she saw something almost sinister in her sister's expression. Allison turned to face her uncle directly. As she spoke, her voice had all the sweetness of cake. "Yes, of course, uncle. Perhaps your admirer might like to join us." Allison looked over her shoulder at the man in question and smiled just enough that her dimples appeared. Julia could not help but notice that she also batted her eyelashes.

Two additional pairs of eyes swiveled and were now staring at the man who had yet to introduce himself.

It was not until that moment that Julia was able to have a proper look at him. He was very handsome, but then he did something that made him extraordinary. He returned Allison's smile with one of his own. Julia's heart lurched in her chest. That smile could be deadly. That smile was familiar.

"I am afraid my knee is giving me a bit of trouble," he said. His voice was deep and had a velvety quality Julia had not noticed until now. "But I wouldn't dream of keeping Miss Morgan from experiencing such a thrilling adventure. Being able to hear about the excitement, while being in the very spot it occurred—why, it will feel as if she were there on the exact day it happened. But," he turned to Julia before continuing, "as you have had the privilege of seeing the site once before, might you be willing to aid me, Miss Julia, in selecting some pastries from the table? With my injury, I am afraid I have lost the use of one hand."

All three looked down and discovered the man was carrying a cane.

Julia's eyes flew back to his face. "If my uncle does not object, I would be more than willing to help you, sir."

Before Edward could speak, the stranger said, "How could he object, Miss Julia? I have known your uncle since I was in nappies. Surely, he could not deny an old, crippled friend your company for a short while."

Clearly flustered, Uncle Edward's face grew red, and his cheeks puffed out. The stranger raised an eyebrow, as if daring him to deny their lengthy association. After a minute, Edward regained his composure and nodded. "No, of course not. Julia, you stay here."

Soon, Julia stood next to this handsome stranger, watching the retreating forms of her uncle and sister. Allison looked over her shoulder once, a scowl upon her face. This was followed by a rich laugh from the man standing at Julia's side.

"Your sister has always held to the philosophy that you should do as she says but not as she does. I have little doubt that had I not intervened, it would be you alone going off to listen to that tired, old tale, just as it had been on your last visit, while she stayed here and ate another bonbon." He looked down into Julia's face and studied it for a minute. "You do not remember me any more than your uncle does, do you?" The question was asked with a playful, amused tone.

The voice suddenly sounded so familiar. The man who had first approached them had been serious, but the more playful he acted the more certain Julia became that she did know him—and very well. She was loath to admit she could not give a name, so she hoped that his question had been rhetorical. The growing silence told her it was not. He was going to make her admit it. Her cheeks burned.

"I will tell you what," he said with a twinkle of mischief in his eye. "We will play a game until you can tell me who I am."

"I am not affirming that I do not know who you are, sir." Julia said carefully. She lifted her chin hoping the small act of defiance might convince him she had not forgotten him but was simply choosing not to acknowledge their association. "But I am very fond of games, and I am in need of distraction."

"As you always have been," he said warmly. "That was your first clue. Now the rules are simple. I give you a clue, and you make a guess. If your guess is incorrect, you must take a bite of one of those delectable sweets from that table. You can take minuscule nibbles if you must, but a bite is required. Then, I will give you another clue."

What an unusual forfeit. Julia's mouth watered at the thought of eating one of the desserts, but she knew she should not. Her dresses for London had already been made and she could not risk out growing them. "And what is my reward if I guess correctly?" she asked.

"When you guess correctly, I will answer one question of your choosing."

"If I had consumed a larger breakfast, I would identify you this very moment, for of course I know who you are, but I am able to survive a small bite of the parfait so I will guess you are the Prime Minister."

She accepted his proffered arm, and they walked toward the table. "I am not the Prime Minister, as I suspect you know, but I am impressed you have heard use of the term."

They reached the table, and Julia's eyes widened as she scanned the array of options.

"If you are looking for a parfait, I recommend this one here. It is divine."

"What made you come over and rescue me from my uncle?" Julia asked.

"I will only answer your questions once you say my name."

Julia lifted a small glass bowl and spoon from the table and took a bite of the dessert. She closed her eyes as the sweetness touched her tongue. She swallowed. "I believe I am owed another clue," she said.

"First, you must tell me if you agree with my assessment of that dessert."

She nodded. "It is wonderful."

"I myself am familiar with the term Prime Minister because I have spent a considerable amount of time visiting Parliament over the past two years. Soon, I will be expected to assume a role in government."

Julia studied the man. Perhaps he looked familiar because she had seen a sketch of him in her father's news sheets, but she could think of no reason why such a person might know who she was. "I know perfectly well who you are, but find I am enjoying this dessert so much, I will simply take another bite."

He chuckled. "I'm glad to hear it. I will confess. I heard Allison attempting to keep you from trying one of these after I had witnessed her eating no less than four bonbons. She was being cruel."

"No good of himself does a listener hear. Speak of the devil and he doth appear."

The man nodded. "Well, Julia, I will count myself fortunate then, for I was not the topic of your conversation with your sister."

"What gives you leave to call me and my sister by our Christian names?"

"Under what circumstances do you think I might form such a habit?"

"I can only assume you knew us when we were children."

He nodded. "And that is your next clue."

Julia's brow furrowed in concentration. She focused on the glass bowl, carefully arranging another spoonful. She lifted her head and stared at the man's features. After a sharp intake of air, she drew her hand to her mouth. Her surroundings grew hazy, and she became lightheaded. "Phillip?" she whispered.

Chapter Three

"Julia?" One of Phillip's hands had a firm grasp on her elbow, another was securely fastened to her waist. "Are you unwell?"

She could hear the words, but they were distant, as if she was in a dream. A wonderful, blissful dream. There was a heavenly smell of musk mixed with sandalwood. She was not sure what it was exactly, but she knew it smelled masculine. The warm, strong bed that supported her felt custom made for her body.

"Do you have any smelling salts?" he continued.

Smelling salts? Her mind processed the question. *Who was that speaking?* The dream began to lift, and her mind flooded with the memories of the last ten minutes. *Of course, he thinks I am going to faint.* She took a deep breath and concentrated until the world came back into focus. She was no ninny and would give him no reason to suspect otherwise. As the gardens stopped spinning and she steadied on her feet, she became aware of his hands and the warmth that emanated from them. Instinctively, she stepped away and his hands fell to his sides. She looked at him and opened her mouth to speak. Words of rebuke formed, but before they left her mouth, she looked at his face. She could not help but notice that his eyes were filled with concern and confusion. How had she not recognized him? He really had not changed much at all. "I apologize. Your knee," she said pointing to his leg. "You should not be expected to support me when you need support yourself."

Phillip raised an eyebrow, then looked down at his leg. "Ah, yes," he said before a small laugh escaped him. "I trust you to keep this confidential, but I do not actually have an injury. The cane is merely an accessory. I saw an opportunity to put it to good use by allowing it to provide us with a reason to be excused from your uncle's company." He reached over and collected the cane which had been resting against the edge of the table.

"When did you set that down?" Julia asked.

"Just before I attempted to steady you. I believe you may have lost consciousness temporarily." He picked up Julia's trifle from the table and handed it to her. "I also took this from you. You looked as though you might drop it."

She took the bowl and gazed at it. She was no longer hungry.

"I want to see you finish that, Julia," Phillip said in a stern tone. "I suspect you have eaten nothing but a light breakfast, and that is why you now appear so pale and lightheaded."

She could hear her father's words. An image of the portrait that hung in the hall flashed through her mind—a perfect daughter and her. The muscles in her face tensed, and she ignored the dish in her hand.

Phillip smiled. "Do you recall the day we built a fort behind the fields?"

Julia did remember. She had raced the Heartford boys toward the woods. Allison was nowhere in sight because she found it undignified to run. The tall shafts of grain hid the dirt path. She had felt so excited. For the first time, she could not imagine her father being able to find her. She was free.

"I'd tried to convince you to climb the tree and help me scout for the ideal location, but you refused. I can still remember, all these years later, you wore that exact same expression." Gently, he pushed her hand and its contents back toward her. "I do not care if you feel hungry. You need something to eat, and this is available." He gave her a look that made her feel like a warm blanket had just been wrapped around her shoulders. In a voice that made her feel safe he said, "It is wrong of your father and sister to make you feel you must go hungry."

Julia's eyes widened as her mind replayed the conversation he had overheard in its entirety. It was one thing having her father imply her figure was full, but it was another matter entirely for him to hear this criticism. "You should not listen to other people's conversations, Mr. Heartford." Warmth flooded her. *I should have heeded Allison's advice and not spoken so openly in company.*

"Yes. I believe you provided me with the same advice not five minutes ago. But," he said with a cheeky grin, "how else would I have known Allison wished to indulge your uncle while you did not?" His smirk belied his words.

The happiness she had been enjoying gave way to discomfort brought on by exposure and humiliation. Her hands gripped her elbows. "I do not require your pity, Mr. Heartford."

"Now, Julia. Did I say I pitied you?"

There really was no need. Everyone pities me. "And that is another thing," she said lifting her chin and looking down her nose at him, "it has been over five years since we have last seen you, Mr. Heartford. I do not see how you can believe it is appropriate to continue to refer to my sister and me by our Christian names."

He straightened and cleared his throat. "Of course, you are right. I was simply so delighted to discover old friends I fell into a habit formed in my youth. Please, forgive me."

"Only if you tell me why you are here."

His posture again relaxed. "There is my friend— the one that drives a hard bargain." He reached into the pocket of his overcoat and withdrew a snuffbox. He opened it and extended it toward Julia, offering her some of its contents.

Julia's face scrunched up. "I do not take snuff," she said curtly.

"I did not think you would," he replied. "I am trying to stop myself. I have traded in the snuff for these small, hard candies that are sold by a confectioner near my home in London." His hand nudged forward, bringing the box a little closer to her, but she shook her head.

"You are avoiding my question, Mr. Heartford."

He sighed, took a candy from the box, and returned the container to his pocket. "My family's ancestral estate abuts your own home, Miss Julia. Surely, you did not expect I should never return. And, as you must know, if you are within the vicinity of Kent when the Everlys host their annual garden party, you would be hard pressed to pass on an invitation."

The response had not been satisfying. "But why have you returned to your estate now, after so many years?" she demanded.

"I believe the rules of our game allowed you to ask a single question, Miss Julia."

"I did not initially ask the question you answered. You offered an explanation on your own to earn my forgiveness."

"I must point out; you did ask a question before then… something involving my cane. As my obligation has been fulfilled, if you wish to hear more, you must barter. I want you to finish that trifle, yet you have blatantly ignored my counsel. I will answer another question after you finish eating."

Julia frowned as she lifted the spoon. Moments later, as the fourth bite entered her mouth, she walked to the table and set down the empty dish. Swallowing, she spun around to face

Phillip. "What specifically brought you back here after all these years?"

Phillip sighed and ran a hand through his hair. "I am sorry that I did not send word to you after I had left. I could have reached out to your father and maintained our friendship. But I was overcome with Johnathan's death, and all of the new responsibilities thrust upon me. I told myself I would set things right between us when we returned, but my parents could not stay here without being reminded of him, so we never came back."

"I did not ask why you cut me out of your life, I asked you to reveal the reason for your return."

"Yes." His eyes darted about, and he put his hands in his pockets. "I have been informed it is time for me to find a wife. Having frequented many events these last few seasons, I have determined that I am not well-suited with the ladies of the *ton*. I have returned home to see if I can fare better here."

Julia tried to swallow but found her mouth had gone dry. At last, she found her voice and asked, "You have left London to find a match? There cannot be more than a dozen possible options here."

Phillip nodded. And then he did the strangest thing. He studied her. His stare was so intense, she felt as if she had been stripped to her chemise. "Miss Morgan, you and I have always been very close. I came to this party today in hopes of finding you. I prayed we might find an opportunity for a private conversation."

His eyes grew dark. It added to his allure, but something was very wrong. His features lost all animation. A part of him had suddenly gone into hiding, leaving behind a shadow of the boy she remembered. Julia no longer wondered why she had not known him instantly.

"We were once like brother and sister. I have always

22

trusted you to keep what I've said in strict confidence. May I once again speak to you about a very sensitive subject?"

Julia was unable to speak, so she nodded her assent.

"I have returned to ask for your sister's hand in marriage."

Julia blinked. Her shoulder sagged, and she expelled a breath of air. "A-Allison?" she stammered. She should have known. *Of course, he had returned for Allison. Wasn't that why they all came? If only it wasn't Phillip.*

Phillip looked away. "Yes. I know that when we were younger, she was partial to Johnathan, but that was long ago." Slowly, he looked back at her. His face which was so full of life only moments before was now unreadable. "Do you know if her heart is currently engaged by anyone special?"

Julia weighed her words. If she were being honest, she would argue that Allison was very much enamored with herself, but Phillip Heartford would not be the first man to find himself taken in by her sister's beauty. Julia had learned long ago that no good would come from speaking such truths. "Although she has been approached by many suitors, I do not believe there were any that she admires. And," she paused, feeling the guilt of betraying her sister's humiliating circumstances, "this is her third season."

He let out a long breath. A gentle smile softened each of his features. "My heart rejoices at the thought I may someday call you my sister, Julia."

The last vestiges of hope were now destroyed. The fantasy that she might one day find a husband she could love now lay entirely in tatters. She reminded herself of the cozy little cottage she was going to acquire—her comfortable life of solitude. But these thoughts which had helped her ignore the empty dance cards and the snickers, did nothing to dull this devastating pain. What was worse, she felt powerless under his spell. She would have done anything for him in that moment. Just as she would have done anything for him five years earlier when she was but a girl of fourteen. She had thought his hold over her had been lost when he left without any word and acted as though she did not exist. But then again, she believed he had broken her heart. Now, hearing his words, knowing she would do all she could to ensure his happiness including helping him in his quest to earn Allison's love, she understood that he had not broken her heart all those years ago. For if he had, why was the feeling she had now far worse than anything she had ever experienced?

"I will do all I can to help," she said. With effort, she pulled her lips upward into a weak smile, hoping it would adequately disguise her pain.

But her disguise was unnecessary. He was no longer looking at her. His gaze was fixed on the hillside's ridge.

Slowly, reluctantly, Julia followed his gaze. There was Allison. Her pale green dress billowing out behind her as she crested the hill and gracefully floated toward them. She was flawless.

"Thank you," he said hastily.

Chapter Four

Dinner at the Morgan household was a quiet affair. There was the usual tinkling of glass, the sound of cutlery at work, and the occasional resonating gong from a lid that had been lifted from a serving dish ever so clumsily. But conversation was generally kept to a minimum. It was for this reason that when Mrs. Morgan spoke, she became the center of attention.

"Did you enjoy the garden party?" she asked as she took a roll from the basket and gave the servant a small nod to inform him her needs had been met. The question had not been directed to anyone in particular, which added greatly to the confusion surrounding this extraordinary event. But Mrs. Morgan did not appear to mind the delay in receiving a response. She buttered her roll and waited patiently.

Mr. Morgan set down his glass. One can only guess that he had grown emboldened by his wife's question, for he cleared his throat and asked, "Did you run into your Uncle Edward, Allison? He has been keen to introduce you to some friends of his."

"Yes, I did have the pleasure of seeing him and meeting his friends," Allison said.

"And what were your thoughts?" their father prodded.

Julia noted the exchange with interest. To ask not one but two questions—why, speculation created by such unusual behavior abound.

Mrs. Morgan looked up from her plate and turned to her

husband. "Do you mean our daughters were introduced to the Duke of Hastingridge? If gossip is to be believed, his heir is not yet attached. He could prove to be an important connection."

"If gossip is to be believed, Mama, his heir is not attached for many reasons, none of which recommend him for the role of husband," Allison said quickly.

"Well, one should not believe everything one hears," Mrs. Morgan said defiantly. "For instance, you have rejected so many offers, there is now false conjuncture about you. I cannot imagine what you are waiting for, but if you wait much longer, you may miss every opportunity."

Mr. Morgan cleared his throat. He summoned the servant carrying the dish of potatoes over. As his plate filled, he turned to Julia. "And what of you, love? Did you meet your uncle's friends? I am sure such a man would know many interesting young people. Some of which might not even be surrounded by a cloud of rumors and innuendo."

"Julia stayed behind," Allison replied.

Mrs. Morgan raised both eyebrows. If Allison had hoped to redirect her mother toward another target, she had succeeded. "Why, whatever for?"

"Actually Mother, you will not believe who we encountered at the party," Julia said. She could feel the smile take hold of her face. She set her napkin in her lap. She could feel excitement trying to burst through her chest.

Mrs. Morgan's face puckered ever so slightly as if she had just eaten something sour. "Unless it was an eligible prince, I do not imagine the encounter would have been worth passing on such a valuable introduction."

"It was an old friend," Julia beamed. "Surely, you must agree that that is better than even a Duke."

Mr. Morgan snorted and shook his head. He turned

back to his plate, mumbling, "At least one of them has some sense."

"It was Mr. Heartford. He has returned at last to spend some time at Marymoor," Allison explained.

"Indeed?" Mrs. Morgan asked. A smile spread over her face. "I agree. Sometime reestablishing old friendships is even more important than forming new ones." A twinkle appeared in her eyes and she looked at Julia with a triumphant smile.

Julia could nearly read her mother's thoughts. Since he had spoken with her, her mother had incorrectly assumed that she was the object of his interest. *A mother's love is blind.* She longed to explain he was here for Allison, but she would not. She had said she would help him, and she had not yet assessed Allison's feelings toward the man. Certainly, her parents would be pleased if either of their daughters married a Heartford. *At least Allison will not disappoint them.*

"Ah," their father said lifting his head ever so slightly before taking a bite of food. The sound was sufficient to inform Julia she was forgiven for her foolish error in judgement, and it was a signal that this experiment was now at an end. Mr. Morgan had spoken—it was time that they resume their meal in the comfort of silence.

The following morning, Julia sat near the window embroidering. Her needle pierced the fabric, and a long thread of silk slid through the opening she had created. It was not until the thread had been pulled all the way through and was securely in place that Julia noticed it was the wrong color. She had just finished a rosebud and had moved onto the leaves, but she had neglected to switch skeins. She sighed as she pulled the pink thread back out. She was frustrated, not because of her small error, which was easily rectified, but because she was fighting to resist her mind's attempt to guide her down a thorny path that would lead to nothing but heartache.

The family had just finished breakfast and, with the exception of Mr. Morgan, had retired to the morning parlor. In past years, the small room would be crowded with callers—each suitor vying for her sister's attention. But eventually, all wells run dry. Between the hearts Allison had bruised and the indulgence her parents had shown for her fickleness, now even Julia's prospects were impacted. But Julia did not mind. Her desire to marry had died years ago and she was grateful Allison appeared to be in no particular hurry. It made things less lonely. Although spinsterhood sounded far more appealing if done in pairs, Allison would marry someday. She decided to simply be happy it had not already happened.

"I sent a letter to my sister Anne, this morning," Mrs. Morgan said. "With the new developments happening here, I thought Julia should stay here a bit longer."

Allison, who had been reading by the fire, set down her cup of tea before placing a mark in her book and closing it. Her gaze focused in on her mother.

Julia's heart felt lighter. She had been dreading spending part of the season in town. It had been bad enough attending local balls and assemblies. She could only imagine the ridicule and embarrassment she would face appearing alongside the *ton*.

"What developments?" Allison asked.

"Why, Mr. Heartford has returned to Marymoor." Mrs. Morgan said it as if the answer was so obvious, she could not comprehend why the question had been asked. She turned to her youngest daughter. "You had hoped to avoid London, and it looks as though you may not need to go there to find your husband."

Julia nearly stabbed herself with her needle. She looked up from her embroidery. "No, Mama. You misunderstand. Mr. Heartford has not returned for me."

With a wave of her hand and a knowing smirk, Mrs. Morgan dismissed her daughter's statement. "Your uncle told your father that he did not recognize him, and apparently neither did anyone else. He did not mingle, socialize, or greet anyone at that party other than you, Julia. I would be willing to bet my mother's pearls that he will be paying us a call this morning."

Before Julia could respond, her sister spoke.

"But do you not think it would be better to allow Julia to explore all of her options?" Allison asked. "Should she not at least attend a few of the events in town?"

"She has repeatedly sworn she prefers not to. Isn't that right, Julia?"

Everyone in the room turned to look at her. Julia wanted to hide.

"I don't wish to explore any options—here or in London," she said. "Mr. Heartford is not interested in me anymore than the men in London will be. This whole process is a waste of money and time. I wish you could just accept, Mama, that no one is going to marry me."

Mrs. Morgan set down her teacup. "Julia, child, don't be ridiculous…"

Before she could say more, the butler walked into the room carrying a silver tray. He approached Mrs. Morgan who looked at the tray with a smile. A calling card and soft words were exchanged before Mrs. Morgan turned to her daughters and said, "It looks as though we will be entertaining a guest this morning."

Sitting up, Julia moved to the edge of her seat. She carefully pushed her needle under several stitches to hold it in place then set the hoop on the table.

Mrs. Morgan looked to Julia as she said, "Our neighbor, Mr. Heartford, from Marymoor has come to call. It seems my pearls are safe."

The doors again opened, and Phillip entered. The women stood, and after proper greetings were made, Mrs. Morgan motioned to her daughters to gather—thus the foursome settled into seats near the fireplace.

"Would you care for some tea, Mr. Heartford?" Mrs. Morgan asked.

"No, thank you. I am afraid I cannot stay long. I have a busy morning." Phillip pulled off his gloves and laid them on his lap.

The doors to the room opened, but this movement did not draw the notice of those in the room. Not until the butler drew near, did Mrs. Morgan look in his direction. He leaned in close and whispered something before retreating. Mrs. Morgan stood. "I do apologize, Mr. Heartford. It appears I am needed for a moment."

Mr. Heartford rose from his seat.

Waving her hand dismissively, Mrs. Morgan said, "Oh, no need for that. I shan't be but a minute. Allison, can you entertain our guest in my stead?"

Allison looked up. "Of course, Mother."

Once Mrs. Morgan left the room, Julia asked, "Have you enjoyed your time back home, Mr. Heartford?"

"It is wonderful to be back, but since my absence lasted for so many years away, I am nearly forgotten." He crossed his legs and leaned back in his chair before continuing. "It is a situation that is entirely of my own doing, but one which I am determined to rectify. This morning I will make several calls in an effort to reestablish my long-forgotten friendships."

"I do not think you are so much forgotten as altered,

Mr. Heartford," Allison chimed in. Her voice had lost the sweetness she normally used when gentlemen callers were present. "When we first encountered you yesterday, I was nearly certain Julia did not recognize you."

Julia's mouth dropped open and she stared at her sister.

"But you did?" he challenged.

"Not at first," Allison admitted. "But I suspect this was by design."

Phillip smiled. "I admit I had hoped to reintroduce myself to our community by making house calls. I prefer speaking with my neighbors individually in a more intimate setting than would be permitted at yesterday's party. But I was not actively hiding my identity. I simply was not advertising it."

Narrowing her eyes, Allison asked, "Not hiding it, hmm?" She took a sip of tea. "I see you have left your cane at home. Am I to assume your knee has made a sudden recovery?"

Julia gasped. "Allison!" she chided. "Mr. Heartford, I apologize. My sister is not herself this morning."

Phillip did not react to Julia's statement. Instead, he stared directly at Allison. "You're more astute than I remember, Miss Morgan. And you are just too quick to assume the worst in people. I do occasionally carry a cane but only as a fashion accessory—not in hopes of concealing my identity, age, or physical fitness."

"Then you did, in fact, have a knee injury?" Allison asked with a raised eyebrow.

Silence permeated the room.

"You simply happened to acquire this injury on the day you were carrying your accessory," she pressed, "and judging by the lack of a cane, you made a full recovery so soon?"

"I merely stated that I had no intention to deceive when

I arrived at the party and made no effort to hide my identity," Phillip explained. "In a spur of the moment decision, I did tell a falsehood regarding my injury. But this falsehood was told only to spare your sister from unpleasantness."

"A lie is a lie, Mr. Heartford. And I do not approve of liars."

"I told you I would not be long." Mrs. Morgan's voice drew the attention of all as she breezed into the room; her lighthearted countenance was at sharp odds with the others in the room. She settled into the seat she had previously enjoyed and turned to her guest. "Now, what were we talking about?"

"Actually," Phillip said, his expression hiding all signs of tension, "I was just about to say my farewell. I have thoroughly enjoyed the visit but am on a very tight schedule this morning. I do hope you will give Mr. Morgan my regards."

Mrs. Morgan pouted. "All ready? That is a shame. I do hope you will consider visiting us again soon."

Phillip stood. "You could not keep me away," he assured her before making his exit.

No sooner had the doors closed than Mrs. Morgan turned to her daughters and said, "Now wasn't that lovely? It must be nice for you both to see the return of your childhood friend."

Julia did not respond. Her eyes were drawn to the chair Phillip had just vacated. Something was there, but what? Suddenly, she knew what she was seeing. *Phillip has left his gloves.* It was as though Providence was giving her the chance she needed to again speak to him alone. She jumped from her chair, grabbed the gloves, and ran from the room. As she hurried toward the front door, she had fleeting thoughts about the propriety of her actions. *What shall I do if the butler is there? How will it look if he is alone?* These thoughts, though present, were harmony to the loud melody that screamed, *he is going about this completely wrong. I must help him.*

It was with relief she found Phillip standing alone in the foyer. When he turned and saw her, his eyes went wide.

"Mr. Heartford, you left your gloves," she said in broken speech. She was panting as she thrust the errant articles toward him.

"Oh. Thank you, Miss Julia." He took the gloves from her hand. "I left my coat with the butler and forgot I had worn the gloves into the parlor."

"Has someone gone to fetch your coat?" Julia turned, looking for a servant.

"Yes, the butler just left to retrieve it," he said, as he put on his gloves.

Julia felt a weight lift from her chest. She could have a private moment with him to say what she needed. "I would again like to apologize for my sister's behavior," she continued.

"Yes. I suppose that could have gone better," he said with a frown.

Julia nodded and scanned the floor around them. She could hear the distinct sound of James's shoes clicking on the marble tiles. Hastily, she looked up and blurted, "Meet me in front of the Adamson's old barn tomorrow at this same hour. I will help you."

Before he could say anything, she ran back to the parlor.

Chapter Five

"Julia, would you help me with my hair?" Allison stood in the doorway brushing her long golden tresses. "Maria had a headache, so I sent her to bed." Without waiting for an answer, she turned and walked away.

After leaving the nursery, the girls had each been given a room of their own, but having grown so accustomed to sleeping together, they habitually found one another in the night. After years of failing to break them of this routine, their parents acquiesced and gave them adjoining bedchambers which were connected by a single door. Julia crossed the room and stepped through the doorway into the pale pink and cream room Allison had occupied since she was seven. Allison took a seat at her vanity and set down the hairbrush. Taking her sister's hair in her hand, Julia began dividing it into sections.

Their eyes met in the mirror. "I cannot believe how rude you were to Mr. Heartford," Julia said. She had been thinking of that morning's encounter all day. She could not decide if she was pleased Allison appeared to dislike the man, or if she pitied him. "You accused him of lying."

"He did lie."

Julia picked up the brush and worked on a section of hair that had managed to get tangled. She did not bother to hold the base of the hair in a firm grasp, and Allison yelped in pain before sending her sister a scowl through the glass messenger.

"Sorry," Julia said. She adjusted her hands in order to minimize her sister's discomfort as she continued to work on the knot. "We all lie on occasion. At least he freely admitted it."

Allison snorted. "I rarely lie within the first few minutes of encountering someone I have not seen in years." She reached over and picked up a necklace lying on the vanity and examined it.

Placing the brush back down, Julia said, "But he did not act out of malice." With agility and speed, she began plaiting Allison's hair. "You were so cold. I thought you were having a difficult morning. But then, you were perfectly charming during Miss James' visit."

With a touch of force, Allison returned the necklace she had been holding to a jewelry box. She lifted her chin and glared at her sister's reflection. "Mr. Heartford has not been involved in our lives for five years." Her voice was raised, and she spoke at a clipped pace. "I see no reason why you are suddenly so keen to invite him to once again be a part of it."

Julia sighed. "He is our neighbor." Having finished a plait, she picked up a pin. "Up or down?"

"Up."

Gathering several more pins, Julia placed the tips in her mouth, holding them with her teeth. She completed attaching the first plait, by carefully inserted a pin into each section of hair and affixing these sections to Allison's scalp. She then took the remaining strands in hand and separated them into groups. "Why would you intentionally try to antagonize our neighbor? Did he do something to you before he left to earn your scorn?"

Allison's eyes flickered up for the briefest of moments. It was purely by chance Julia saw the movement, and the significance of the action was not lost on her.

"He did nothing you would deem unreasonable," Allison said, once her gaze was again safely hidden. "And he has never acted with the intent of hurting me."

Julia's hands stilled. "That does not sound like an answer." With a strength in her voice born from concern, she asked, "What did he do that inadvertently hurt you?"

Shaking her head, Allison replied, "It was nothing. It is simply…" She took a breath and looked up at the ceiling. "Mr. Heartford is a reckless man who acts without considering the consequences to himself or those around him." Her words were broken. It was obvious she was struggling to keep from crying.

This response did little to assuage Julia's growing concern. "We have not seen him for five years, but the anger you feel towards him radiates from you with such intensity." Julia moved so she could look directly into her sister's eyes. "What has he done?"

Allison's eyes filled with tears and a sob escaped her. "He took Johnathan from me!" she choked.

Stunned into silence, it took Julia several seconds to respond. She set down the pins she had been gathering to hold the second plait in place, reached out, and drew Allison into her arms. The heartbroken sobs shook her, and she rubbed her sister's back until they quieted. At last, Allison's breathing returned to normal. Julia let go and straightened herself. Softly, she asked, "Is that why you have not married? Were you in love with Johnathan?"

"No," Allison said as she rummaged through one of the drawers of the vanity. "I *am* in love with Johnathan. I have never stopped." She withdrew a handkerchief from the drawer and dabbed at her eyes.

Julia returned to her place behind her sister. Reaching over and picking up the pins she had set down, she finished with Allison's hair. Allison stood from the small bench.

"Thank you," Allison said as she reached up and touched her hair. She walked to the edge of her bed and sat down.

Julia followed. Without an invitation, she sat down next to her sister and took hold of her hands. "Allison, I am so sorry. I never knew."

"Of course, you didn't." A small laugh escaped Allison, and she gave her sister a smile. "He never knew. I hid it." Allison stood from the bed and walked to her dresser, retrieving the candle snuffer once she arrived. "But it would not have mattered. He was in love with someone else."

"I find that hard to believe," Julia replied. She kept her eyes trained on her sister.

"And yet it is true. Men may notice me because I am pretty, but what they really want is a woman like you." Allison walked to those candles that lay farthest from the bed and began extinguishing the flames.

"You are wrong," Julia said, shaking her head. "No man will ever want me. How could they even see me when I stand next to you? I am sure he was not immune to your charms."

"You do not see your own worth." Allison walked by the mirror and paused to glance at her reflection. She fixed a pin. "Besides, I heard him speak of his love before his death."

Julia's eyes grew wide, and she stared at her sister in disbelief. "He spoke to you of such matters?"

With all but those candles in the two chambersticks closest to the bed smothered, Allison set the snuffer down and walked back to the bed. "No. He was speaking to Phillip of it in the woods. I happened to overhear them." She sat down next to Julia with tears again gathered in the corners of her eyes poised to roll down her cheeks. "I became so angry, I begged God to punish him. When he died—"

"You cannot blame yourself," Julia said cutting her off. "You were not responsible."

"I do not blame myself. I blame Phillip," Allison snapped. "He was the fool who put himself in danger! He should have known how Johnathan would react if anything happened."

Julia stiffened. "You cannot blame Phillip for his brother's death." She shook her head. "It was an accident. It was not his fault any more than it was yours."

"It was an accident that would have never occurred if Phillip hadn't walked onto that lake." Allison's tone left no room for debate. "I was there. Johnathan told him that the ice was thinning. He told him not to go, but Phillip didn't listen. He never listens to anyone." The tears spilled out the edges of her eyes. She returned to the vanity and retrieved her handkerchief. She blew her nose then walked back and sat down on the bed. "If he had not been so careless, Johnathan would still be here."

Julia held her sister tight. She gently stroked Allison's back until the crying stopped.

"What happened to Johnathan is a tragedy. I believe Phillip also blames himself. But you are both wrong. It was an accident. No one forced Johnathan to attempt to save him." Julia spoke as one might to a frightened child. "They both suffered. It is natural to be angry that one should survive while the other did not."

Allison pulled away. The anger that had blazed in her eyes moments before had cooled, but the smoldering embers were not fully extinguished. "Oh, Julia, do you love him? I do not know if I could stand having him as a brother. He never thinks of how his actions will impact those around him."

"N-no!" Julia stammered. "Me? What would make you think I loved him? Why would you think he might ask me to marry him? That is simply preposterous. I could never do such a thing. You know I have my heart set on a little cottage where

I can live alone."

"It's just he obviously wanted to speak to you alone yesterday, and then he came calling today. You were very close to one another when we were children."

"Well, I am no longer a child, and I hardly know the man. Besides, I am very certain you will not need to worry about him seeking my hand. He said he has always viewed me as a sister."

"Did he?" Allison's eyes narrowed. She turned and fluffed her pillows. "I just remembered. I also dislike that he lies. Like he did with his supposed injury."

"I confess," Julia said as she worried her hands, "I did not know of your dislike and could not have dreamed it ran so deep. But surely, you must know it is irrational and unhealthy to hold onto the belief he is responsible for Johnathan's death. Even if only for your own well-being, you must try to let go of such a notion." Julia rose from the bed and took one of the chambersticks in hand. She walked toward the door leading to her room, but after a few steps, she stopped and turned. "You must let Johnathan go. You cannot live your life in the past. You must look to the future."

Allison had climbed under the covers. She leaned over and blew out the small flame near her bed. Hidden in the darkness, she said, "While what you say may be true, I see no reason I should include Phillip as part of that future."

"You needn't, but you must learn to stop blaming him. It is unfair to him, and it is a sign that you haven't accepted what has occurred. Besides, it looks as though he intends to spend more time at Marymoor." The soft glow of Julia's candle illuminated her bedroom, allowing her to avoid a collision with the boots she had left sitting in the middle of the floor. "Spending time with Mr. Heartford will help you find the closure you need."

Allison sat up. "It is so hard," she called. "He has Johnathan's eyes, and his stance is so similar. When I was returning—after I'd left Uncle Edward—I walked over the ridge and thought I was seeing a ghost."

"Do you want to move on, Allison? Do you want to find a husband who can make you happy and live a full life?"

There was a pause, and Julia wished she had stayed near the bed so she might better read her sister's expression. "I do, but I am afraid. If I spend time with Phillip and do not feel anger, then I will be filled with pain. And..." She paused. As the seconds passed, Julia began to think her sister would remain silent. "It seems wrong to live my life when Johnathan never had that chance."

Julia opened the door enough to slip back into Allison's room. She set her chamberstick on the table near the door and leaned against the door jam. "Do you think he would want to see you throw away your life because he lost his?"

"I don't know."

"Well, he was my friend as well." Julia tried to stifle a yawn with minimal success. "I think he would have wanted to see you live your life enough for the both of you."

"I don't even know how." Allison's voice sounded small and lost in the big, dark room.

Without even being aware of her movement, Julia glided across the space between them and discovered herself sitting on the edge of her sister's bed, holding her hands. "You need to move on. That doesn't mean forgetting him. It means acknowledging and working through the pain you have never dealt with." The flame on the candle Julia had left near the door flickered—sending a small beam of light in their direction. Allison's cheek was illuminated. It glistened—a sure sign it was damp. Julia reached over and wiped it with the pad of her thumb.

Allison laughed. "And how am I supposed to do that?"

"I do not know for sure," Julia responded. She wanted to reassure Allison and hoped her tone had made up for her lack of advice. "But I think learning to spend time with Phillip—without the anger or the pain—would be a start."

Allison rolled onto her side. "I will think about it." Allison sounded exhausted and emotionally drained.

She needs her rest. Julia again stood and walked into her room, collecting her candle on the way. Once more, the heavy door creaked as it was pushed shut. Just before the latch touched the strike, Julia said softly, "That is all I ask," but she could not say if her words had been heard or if her sister had already fallen to sleep.

Chapter Six

Julia listened to the birds sing as she walked down the weathered path to the old barn. The walk was not the pleasant, peaceful stroll she had expected. Since the barn had not been in use in decades, the roads that led to it had long ago ceased to receive any sort of maintenance. In fact, the path she now walked could have been missed altogether if one did not know to look for it. The turn off from the main road was practically hidden by fallen branches and weeds, all of which continued to create obstacles at periodic intervals throughout her journey. The trees overhead created a canopy of leaves, effectively blocking out the sun's rays. Not only did this leave the path dark, but the soil remained slightly damp despite the absence of any rain for a full five days. While damp soil did not pose a real threat, small patches of rather slick mud hid in the lower lying areas. Julia had to tread carefully to avoid slipping.

It is fortunate I am an avid walker. Allison could never navigate this path without experiencing at least two falls.

As her distance from the main road grew, the enormity of what she was doing began to sink in. After breakfast, Allison had pulled her aside and lectured her on the dangers of impropriety. She had been reminded that, unless she was in a public space, she should never place herself in a position to be left alone—especially with an unmarried man. And here she was, heading to a remote area for a clandestine meeting which she herself had arranged.

She immediately dismissed thoughts of Phillip acting in

an untoward manner. But as Allison had said, those rules were not in place simply for the purpose of protecting her reputation. They were also intended to ensure her safety. How could she know if this barn was safe? The barn was so isolated, it would be ideal for a troop of bandits. What if she came upon them while they slept late after an exhausting evening of thieving and pillaging? Would she be harmed, taken prisoner, or worse? Or, what if the barn was now infested with rabid rats? Julia slowed her approach as her mind considered all of the possibilities.

A twig snapped a few feet behind her. The sound gave her such a start, she stepped forward without looking at the terrain. Her shoe landed on a small pocket of mud and her leg slid forward. As soon as she lost control of her footing, she knew she could not regain her balance. She closed her eyes, bracing herself for the inevitable. But rather than feeling the cold hard surface of the ground slamming against her body, she felt a pair of warm and soft, yet strong, arms as they caught her body. She opened her eyes as she was being righted. Once again, she stood face to face with Phillip Heartford.

With as much dignity as she could muster, she curtsied and mumbled, "Mr. Heartford."

He returned the greeting and tipped his hat. She attempted to ignore the bemused smile on his face, but her efforts were thwarted when he quipped, "You need to stop making a habit of falling into my arms, Miss Julia."

Heat filled her cheeks. She could feel her teeth grinding against one another but made a conscious effort to stop herself. This habit had, on occasion, caused her jaw to ache. She resumed walking and he fell in step beside her.

"But I seem to have frightened you," he added, as if he could see his efforts to lessen her discomfort had had the opposite impact. "I apologize."

"No need, Mr. Heartford. You only startled me." A squirrel carrying a nut in its mouth ran across the path and dove into the underbrush. It showed no signs of rabies. "If I was frightened," Julia said reflectively, "it was by my own overactive imagination."

Phillip rubbed his chin. "I do seem to recall a little girl who insisted she would one day become the fairy queen." He turned slightly and examined her back. "But I do not see, and did not feel, any wings on your back when I caught you just now." They came to an overturned tree trunk, and Phillip offered his assistance. "Does that mean you are still just a fairy apprentice?"

"Thank you," Julia said as she accepted his help and gingerly stepped over the barrier. Once the obstacle was cleared, Julia lifted her chin and said in a regal voice, "I was never *just* a fairy apprentice, sir. I was *the* fairy apprentice."

Phillip had the decency to at least look contrite. "Of course, I meant no offense, fairy apprentice," he said while executing an extravagant bow.

With a lift of her eyes, Julia informed him he had permission to rise. "But," she said, maintaining her air of dignity, "I decided that my skin is too fair for the life of a fairy. They do, after all, spend a considerable amount of time outdoors."

With a solemn nod, Phillip replied, "Yes, I can imagine that might deter many an English maiden from pursuing such an opportunity. And there is no denying it would be a terrible shame to damage your perfect complexion."

Julia lowered her face, knowing his comment had caused her to blush, but her gaze remained fixed on Phillip. He looked away from her, but his neck had grown red. She wondered if he'd realized the inappropriate nature of his comment.

He hastily added, "Have you considered any alternative occupations?"

Julia knew this pattern. He had discovered his faux pas and was attempting to direct her attention elsewhere. "Humm," she said pretending to ponder the question. "I had briefly toyed with the possibility of becoming a dragon slayer, but then I discovered that someone has already rid these woods of the terrible beasts."

Phillip laughed. "Yes, so I did."

Julia caught sight of an exposed tree root just in time to circumvent the obstacle. When Phillip then extended his arm, she took hold, reasoning that this path had grown more treacherous with time and accepting help was far less humiliating than a second tumble.

"Then I am to take it," he asked as his eyes swept the surrounding area, "that after my final valiant battle to save our lands, the dragon lair was never repopulated?"

"No. Such a thing requires the strength of many strong imaginations," Julia conceded. "Mine alone was insufficient to entice them to return to the area." Despite the obvious dangers posed by such creatures, Julia could not keep a hint of disappointment out of her voice. "Actually, when you left, a great many mythical creatures died in these parts."

"What a shame. Now that our homesteads are so ordinary, it sounds as if we too will need to abandon the follies of youth and assume the roles of proper adults."

Julia smoothed her dress by running her hands down its length. "Well, yes. That is why we are meeting today, is it not?" Her tone, much like her mood, no longer held any playful undertones. "You intend to marry, and I am here to help you. If that is not a step toward adulthood, I cannot say what is."

"Actually, I did not come here today to obtain your advice on courting the fair princess. I came because your request to meet was far too bold." He stopped walking, and she followed suit. "You must be more careful, Julia."

Julia felt her muscles strain as her jaw clenched and eyes narrowed. She removed her hand from his sleeve and folded her arms across her chest.

"Now, do not be angry," he continued. "Your sister is in her third season. While I hope to soon have her married, this is hardly common knowledge. And though it should not, the fact Allison has not yet secured a husband reflects badly on you. You must do nothing further to hurt your opportunities to find a good match."

"I cannot see how this is any of your concern, Mr. Heartford." Julia began marching forward. With a few long strides, Phillip was again by her side. She did not look at him but snapped, "You sound like my father."

"I prefer to think of myself as a brother."

His words were spoken with such warmth and affection Julia felt her anger ebbing away. She was immediately annoyed with herself for forgiving him so easily. He had just criticized her for being here when he himself was doing precisely the same thing. Further, she was only here because she wanted to help him. Yet, if she were being honest with herself, she would admit she had always found it difficult to stay upset at him for long.

She gave him a sideways glance and the edges of her lips lifted slightly. "And when did this brotherly affection develop?" she asked. "I do not recall feeling so well protected when you pushed me into the lake or," she moved her reticule to the arm farthest from him, "when you left a snail for me in my purse."

He rubbed the back of his neck. "I'm sorry. I forgot how horrible I have been on occasion." He slipped his hands into the pockets of his breeches.

Julia giggled and once again placed her hand on his arm. She was rewarded with a warm smile.

"But to answer your question," Phillip continued, "I guess my desire to protect you happened while I was away. I grew up during that time. I came to see what a self-centered child I had been. In doing so, I came to understand where in this world my place is."

She raised an eyebrow and looked at him askance. "And you believe your place involves acting as my brother?" The incredulity she felt was more than evident in her tone.

"Precisely," he said.

She cleared her throat. "Well, if you hope to make that our official relationship, I suggest you set aside your brotherly concern for a moment and listen to what I have to say. If you do not, you will sooner see my sister's hand on your cheek than on your arm." Julia stepped on a rock that protruded from the surface. Her grip on Phillip tightened briefly until she was no longer in danger of stumbling.

They rounded a bend. The dark path opened onto a very small, overgrown field. The remains of a dilapidated barn stood before them. The structure should have appeared out of place in this wild enclave inhabited solely by Mother Nature, but time had not been kind, and in its dilapidated state, it now looked more natural than man made. Any evidence of paint had long since washed away. More boards had fallen to the ground than remained nailed to the frame. Vines snaked up what was left of the west wall of the structure.

"Well, we are here now, so I see no reason to rush away," Phillip said. "But I would prefer not to venture much closer. The building no longer looks sound."

"What a pity. I wonder where the ghost will live," Julia said to herself.

"Pardon?"

"Oh. I was just remembering when we were children. We hid here from Johnathan and Allison. Do you remember?" she asked.

"Yes. I knew Johnathan would never look for us here. He thought the building would fall over any second and that it was unsafe to enter. I cannot say he was wrong."

"Well, Allison believed this barn was haunted. That was how I knew she would not dare look for us." Julia's eyes lit up as she studied the eerie remains.

"Were you frightened?" Phillip asked.

"Oh no. I came back every day for a week hoping to meet the ghost, until I concluded she must have moved. If it had looked like this back then, I think she might have remained." Julia took a few steps toward the barn. Phillip reached out toward her. Before his hand touched her, Julia spun around. Looking at his outstretched arm, she giggled. "Don't worry. I shall keep my distance." Julia looked directly into his dazzling eyes and said, "Do you know, if I had been afraid of ghosts, I would not have been afraid when we hid. I can never be afraid when I'm near you."

Phillip blinked and his breathing grew shallow. The tips of his ears turned pink. He remained silent for several minutes while he loosened his tie and nervously paced. After some time, he cleared his throat. "Miss Julia, you had some advice you wished to impart."

Embarrassed, Julia turned toward the barn and said, "You are a busy man. I am sorry for losing myself. As you yourself pointed out, Allison was very fond of your brother, Phillip. She never truly grieved his passing. Naturally, you possess many of his features and mannerisms; therefore, you remind her of what was lost," She allowed herself one moment of self-pity before composing herself and turning back toward Phillip. What she found was a pained visage staring back at her.

"It is not my features or mannerisms that she sees. I killed him." His eyes were dark, and he looked like a shell of the dragon slayer who had walked with her here.

"No. You did not. It was just an accident." Julia stepped close and took his hands in hers. "Allison knows that, but she is hurting. Much like you. I had not seen it until now, but you are right to pick her. You need each other. You can help each other through your mutual grief."

Phillip laughed, and the sound sent a chill down Julia's spine.

Julia could only assume he doubted his ability to win her sister's good impression. She wanted to offer words of encouragement. "She will spend time with you, but you must wait until you are both in less pain before you attempt to court her."

"Are you expecting me to capture her heart?" Phillip asked.

Julia dropped his hands and straightened. "Naturally," she said.

Phillip opened his mouth to speak, but then closed it and looked at her. His eyes shifted upward as if he was contemplating a great puzzle. Finally, he said, "And how am I to find this time to help her work through this grief? Am I to confront her in front of your mother during one of my twenty-minute calls?"

"Actually," Julia beamed, obviously very pleased with herself, "I have thought of that. My sister and I are scheduled to visit the Everlys' hothouse next Wednesday. We will arrive at noon. You were able to maintain correspondence with Mr. Everly's son, and you remain good friends, do you not?"

Phillip nodded and looked at the ground.

"Then you should easily be able to secure an

invitation."

"To tour a hothouse?" he asked.

"Indeed. Allison is very interested in horticulture."

Phillip lifted his gaze, and he wore a grimace on his face. "Horticulture?"

"Yes. I can see from your expression, you do not share this passion, so I suggest you brush up before Wednesday. Now if you will excuse me, Mr. Heartford." Julia curtsied and walked around the perimeter of the barn.

"Wait," he called after her. "Aren't you going home? Don't you want me to accompany you?"

"No. Please do not wait for me," she called back. "I have more business to attend to, but do not fear. I will not approach the barn. I will see you next Wednesday," she replied.

Chapter Seven

It was with no small measure of annoyance Phillip hastily marched down the dark path leading away from the barn.

When I chastised her for arranging a meeting with me, I assumed that this was the first time she had done something so improper. But the way she just sent me off—perhaps meeting with men in the middle of the woods is a frequent and normal occurrence for her. He ground his teeth. *And she held my hands! Why must she do such a thing? And how could she do it with such ease?*

Clenched fists rapidly swung back and forth in unison with each long stride. A flicker of resentment lingered in the back of his mind. Part of him wished to blame Johnathan for putting him in this position, but guilt acted the role of a powerful guard and refused to allow him to recognize any feelings other than anger. As he readied himself to battle the thick brush to gain entrance to the main road, he was struck by a thought. This was the only road toward or away from the barn. If he wanted to discover who she was meeting with, he needed only to wait here and find out.

He scoured his surroundings looking for an inconspicuous place to wait. Unfortunately, in the middle of the woods such a place consisted of a rather small clearing that was obscured behind what appeared to be a prickly bush. It was not ideal, but he would need to make do. He climbed and pushed his way to the clearing, certain he was ruining a perfectly good pair of breeches in the process. A few rebellious thorns managed to find the chink in his armor between his sleeve and his glove. They attacked with venom. Once he had finally reached the clearing, he looked at his wrists to discover several scrapes that itched terribly. Although it had felt as if the bush was twelve feet high when he attempted climb over it, now that he was safely standing in the clearing, he acknowledged it did not even quite reach his chest. He would need to crouch in an uncomfortable position to avoid notice. An internal dispute began over when he should assume this pose, but the sound of Julia's humming put an end to the debate. He tangled himself into a ball and thanked the heavens that his irritation had sped his journey down the path, giving him just enough time to concoct and execute this plan.

Much to Phillip's chagrin and annoyance, Julia did not stop on the path. She continued on to the main road. When she had claimed that she had business to attend to, that business was apparently not at this location. So why hadn't she wanted him to escort her? And how was he going to extract himself from this mess before he lost sight of her? Her humming was growing fainter, and he could tell it was coming from the direction leading to her house. If he could hear her humming, would she be able to hear the snapping of twigs, scraping of thorns, and shaking of leaves that was inevitable once he attempted to extricate himself from his current position?

I will simply need to be careful.

With the grace of an elephant, Phillip managed to break free from his thorny prison and was soon on the main road. Julia could not have felt significant alarm over the ruckus he had made, for she failed to investigate and was now no longer in sight.

He hurried down the road attempting to dust himself off as he went. He heard the faint sound of a female voice and slowed his pace. Quietly, he edged forward. The voice was Julia's. He stopped. Although the road gently curved and this feature had enabled him to stay out of sight thus far, if he proceeded any further, he would be in her line of sight. A second voice reached his ear. It was that of a young girl.

"Please, Miss Julia, we don't think it is right to take all of your money. What will you use to live?"

The sweet tinkling of Julia's laugh echoed through the woods. "You need not worry, Emma. This is just my pin money. My father gave it to me for buying unimportant things like ribbons or lace. I do not need it, and I wish to give it to you."

"Won't he be angry if you don't return with the ribbons or lace?"

"I promise he won't even notice. And if it makes you feel better, next week, I will keep a little for myself. I can use it to buy a bit of candy, and if you promise not to tell your mother, I will share some with you. Now, take this and run along. A lady should never be this far from home without a chaperone."

The little girl giggled and said goodbye. Julia's humming resumed and began to fade. Phillip remained in place, speechless.

Chapter Eight

Caleb James leaned forward, placed his arms on his desk, and studied Phillip Heartford. "You would like to tour my uncle's hothouse?" he asked. A smile of amusement pulled on his features.

"Yes." Phillip reached into his breast pocket and withdrew a small leather-bound book. He opened it to a place marked by a ribbon then flipped a few pages. "My calendar is open next Wednesday if that suits you," he added before shutting the book and returning it to his pocket.

"So confident of your invitation, I am guessing you have already recorded it in your little appointment ledger," Caleb said with a smirk. He picked up a letter opener carved out of ivory, leaned back, and tapped the ivory against the arm of his upholstered chair as he scrutinized Phillip. "May I ask when you suddenly acquired an interest in horticulture? I seem to remember you saying that science was about as exciting as watching grass grow."

Phillip snorted. "Would you believe me if I said a recent battle with some shrubbery has opened my mind to the idea of learning about my enemy?" he asked, pulling up his sleeve and thrusting his wrist forth to display the scratches he had received earlier that day.

"You are a brilliant strategist, and the crown would greatly benefit from your mind should you put it to use against the French forces, but no." Caleb ceased the tapping and placed the tip of the letter opener against his lower lip. "I would, however, believe your request has something to do with my sister's plans to provide a tour that very day to the Morgan girls."

Caleb set the opener back down. He rested his chin on his fist and closed his eyes. A minute later, he opened them and stared across the desk. "I met them—at my uncle's garden party. I remember now! My uncle introduced me to the chubby brunette when I first arrived. The name Morgan rang a bell, but I certainly did not think of you. Then, I was speaking to Fitz's father when a friend of his rushed up and introduced a pretty blond also by the name Morgan."

Phillip concealed a small yawn then said drily, "Yes, I know."

"You know? Do not tell me, you were there." Caleb's eyes narrowed.

"I was. And I made sure to greet your aunt and tell her what a splendid affair it was."

"But you left me there to fend for myself?" Caleb's hand rested on the desk and his fingers tapped against the surface in quick succession. The jaw line of his chiseled face appeared even sharper than before.

Shaking his head, Phillip gave his friend a mocking look of pity. "Did you not have Fitz to entertain you?"

"Of course not." Phillip could tell by Caleb's tone and the flailing of his arms he was genuinely hurt. "He left the day before with the intent to avoid the dreadful thing. Apparently, his reserve bachelor had taken ill and was unable to act as a shield between him and the unmarried ladies in attendance. I cannot believe you did not even say hello."

With a sigh, Phillip said, "It was truly not meant as a slight. I quietly snuck in, stayed in the shadows, and had only attended to get the lay of the land. I really just wanted to observe and reacquaint myself with faces. I had no intention of speaking to anyone, your aunt aside."

"Humm. No intention? Then I take it that while I was not worth receiving your greeting, some young woman was? One of the Morgan sisters I am guessing."

Phillip said nothing, thus confirming the accusation.

A smile returned to Caleb's face. "When we first met and you discovered who my uncle was, you often spoke of this place. I had forgotten until a few moments ago just how often a Julia Morgan was mentioned. There was no mistake that you were smitten. If anyone can understand the lengths to which a man will go for love, it is I. And in terms of your admiration, I can appreciate why you find her so appealing. I take it she is that pretty blond."

"I believe you are thinking of Miss Allison Morgan," Phillip said quietly. "Julia's hair is darker."

"Interesting," Caleb said as he again picked up the letter opener and twirled it with his fingers. His gaze bore into the man across from him. "So, it is Miss Julia that has sparked your sudden fascination for plants."

Phillip averted his gaze. He swallowed. "If you are angry with me for not finding you and visiting at the garden party, I apologize." He rubbed his palms against the legs of his trousers.

Laughing, Caleb shook his head. "You can't possibly think you can escape that easily. For years, you've watched me pine away for Mary. You took great pleasure in teasing and torturing me. The tables have turned my friend, and I intend to enjoy this."

Phillip's mouth grew dry. "How is Miss Walker?" he asked feebly.

"Oh no you don't. Miss Morgan—or is it Miss Julia—I cannot recall which was the elder, she enjoys horticulture, I take it?"

"No. I do not think she enjoys it at all. Miss Julia that is. She is the younger of the two and that is not one of the hobbies that holds her interest. It is her elder sister who is interested in your plants."

"Ah, so while Miss Morgan enjoys the tour, you can help entertain Miss Julia."

Phillip let out a sigh. "No. As I believe I mentioned a long time ago, I have no intention of pursuing a romantic relationship with Miss Julia."

"Miss Julia now, is it? Earlier it was simply Julia."

"Force of habit. We were all childhood friends."

"If you have so little interest in the younger Morgan sister, why are you seeking an invitation to join a tour we are both certain will bore you to tears?"

"I would like to reacquaint myself with Miss Morgan."

"Ha!" Caleb slapped the desk and stood up. "How many times did you mock me because I was initially drawn to Mary's beauty? And here you are, all these years later, returning home only to find that your interesting, funny, imaginative friend is a little homely. Suddenly, your affections shift to her pretty sister."

Phillip's nostrils flared. "She is most certainly not homely!" he snapped. "And my affections have made no such shift. I am only hoping to marry Miss Morgan. While I don't *actively* dislike her, I also have no particular fondness for her. Affection plays no part in this."

Settling back into his chair, Caleb cocked his head to one side and raised an eyebrow. "But judging by your behavior, I will venture to say you do still have some attachment to her sister."

Phillip bent forward and put his elbows on his knees. With his shoulders hunched forward, he shook his head as if he found the ground between his feet very disappointing. "Fine," he said through gritted teeth. "Yes, I do. I admit, I once fancied myself in love with Miss Julia, but had Johnathan lived, she would have married him." He lifted his head and glared at Caleb. "She was only ever meant to be my sister. I will not take what belongs to my brother just because he is dead. It would disgrace his memory. Besides," he said, breaking eye contact and snorting while shaking his head, "she loved him all along. When she looks at me now, all she sees is shadows of him." He sighed. "I want her to be a part of my life, but I am no longer the selfish child I was when we met. I understand that my role in her life is as a brother, not a husband." His voice dropped until it was nearly inaudible. "Marrying Miss Morgan means I can still protect Julia, and her prospects for marriage will be enhanced once her elder sister marries."

Caleb's expression implied he thought Phillip a madman. "May I summarize what I have just heard? As I understand it, you blame yourself for your brother's death so you are punishing yourself by marrying a girl you do not particularly care for so you can watch your actual love get married to another?"

"I am not trying to punish myself. It is just that I accept that Julia does not feel toward me the way I once believed I felt toward her." Slouching in his chair, Phillip's chest tightened as he thought about what he was about to say. "I want her to marry someone she loves. And while I am not such a man, I can give her a better chance to find a love match by marrying Allison Morgan—a woman I find no more or less agreeable than any other woman I might marry."

"So, Miss Morgan," Caleb asked in a voice that showed his disbelief, "the very pretty blond, has had no offers and is somehow hurting Miss Julia's marriage prospects?"

Phillip shrugged. "She has not accepted any offers anyway, and she is in her third season. Her parents may not be ready to accept it, but if she does not find a match this season, she will be on the shelf." Knowing that the topic of conversation had drifted away from Julia, Phillip tried to pull himself together. He straightened himself and wiped all traces of vulnerability from his visage. "You know many in our circle will assume there are issues with the family if the older, fairer daughter could not find a match."

"You have no knowledge of why Miss Morgan has been unable to secure a match?"

"No, nor do I particularly care. I have known her long enough to know that I can live with her faults. She loves the country and can stay here, near her family, while I devote most of my time to building my political career."

Caleb shook his head. "Well, if you are determined to marry her, you at least have the upper hand." Caleb glanced to the fire and stood up. He walked over and poked at the log, sending sparks flying up the flue. "You are even eligible to a woman who is not desperate. I am not sure why you want to waste your Wednesday touring our hothouse when you can simply have this business over and done with."

Furrowing his brow, Phillip asked, "What do you mean?"

Caleb turned from the fire and looked into Phillip's eyes. "I mean, what is stopping you from going to her now and asking for her hand?"

"Isn't it expected that I court her first?"

Laughing, Caleb returned the poker to its place on the hearth and walked back to his desk. Once seated, he said, "Perhaps, if you were a hero in a romance novel. But as you are not," he paused and gave his friend a meaningful glance, "you are wasting your time with such nonsense."

Phillip scoffed. "If it is so easy, and I can just go explain to her that she should marry me because I can offer her security and comfort, why have you not gone and requested Mary Walker's hand?"

"Because Mary Walker is not in her third season, out of options, and staring spinsterhood in the eyes." As was often the case when speaking of Mary, Caleb's tone was impassioned. "Besides, I want Mary to be as deeply in love with me as I am with her when we marry. I find the idea of a loveless marriage repulsive; therefore, the idea of marrying her before she's fallen in love with me involves too much risk. What if I discover once it is too late that she can never grow to love me back?" His face fell as he spoke of this hidden fear. He paused and visibly struggled for composure. "But as you do *not* view love as an important component to a union, I do not see your need to wait."

Phillip nodded as he weighed the merits of his friend's argument. *Perhaps, it is best to get this over with. Once my fate is sealed, I will stop entertaining foolish fantasies.* "I see your point," he said at last. "So, you believe I can simply present her with my offer, and she will agree?"

"There is certainly a reasonable chance. But you should first appeal to her father. Help him understand what a precarious position his daughter is now in. He will help you persuade her."

"You do not think it might be better to first spend time with her?"

"I say, if you want to get something done, you start with the easiest approach. Only if that fails do you try a more difficult route. In other words, if you ask and she refuses, you can still try to entice her and then ask again." He tilted his head to one side and swept his arms open, showing the palms of his hands. "At least if you ask first, there will be no confusion about your wooing efforts."

Phillip's face scrunched up. "Pardon?" he asked.

Caleb elaborated further. "Imagine you say nothing. Now, you know you have never been good at masking your emotions. If you simply come to the tour without first revealing your intentions, she will see a man who has an obvious aversion to plants and an affection for her sister. She will assume you are there to spend time with Miss Julia. But if you ask her to marry you tomorrow, one of two things will occur." He paused and leaned forward. Looking Phillip directly in the eyes, he spoke his next words slowly, "If she agrees, you need not waste all that time trying to win her over. If she rejects you, she will know you are enduring the tour for her benefit. Every little effort you make will demonstrate your commitment to winning her heart. It will be even more romantic that you are engaging in things you find distasteful simply to see her."

"Then I have the invitation for Wednesday?"

"You do. And the invitation is not predicated on whether or not you seek her hand in advance. And of course, I will be accompanying the group to protect my sister's honor, and because watching you attempt to pursue a lady promises to be very entertaining."

Phillip stood and extended his hand. The two men shook hands before Phillip walked toward the door. As he left, he called back, "Thank you. I will need to think on your advice."

Chapter Nine

A cold breeze blew past Phillip as he rode through the gates of the Morgans' estate. The weather had been particularly pleasant as of late, but this morning, gray clouds had gathered overhead, creating a somber mood that echoed his own feelings. After years, Phillip had perfected the art of walling off his emotions. Coming back to Marymoor had awoken something in him. If he were being honest with himself, he would know it was Julia that had reached in and touched his heart. But if proper credit had been issued, rather than feeling gratitude, he would have been angry. Now, more than ever before, numbness was his ally. He was about to change the course of his life, and the path he was determined to take was far from pleasant.

He dismounted and tied his horse to a post. He had made no appointment and did not anticipate a lengthy stay. There was no need to send for a groom. Buck could wait right here, ready to carry him away as soon as this ordeal was over. Stroking the side of the animal's neck he whispered, "Well, Buck, wish me luck."

His legs felt heavy as he ascended the stairs to the front door. He knocked, and once greeted, asked that his card be given to Mr. Morgan. He waited, half-hoping that the man was indisposed, but such hopes were dashed when the butler returned, took his coat and hat, and beckoned him to follow.

"Mr. Heartford," Mr. Morgan said to Phillip as he entered the office. "I was sorry to have missed you on your last visit. I have been meaning to come by Marymoor and welcome you home."

The greeting was warm and exuberant. Phillip had always liked Mr. Morgan.

"Thank you," Phillip responded. He had practiced what he wanted to say but had forgotten the need for pleasantries. "I am still in the process of making Marymoor again presentable after my long absence."

"Yes, I can imagine." Mr. Morgan walked toward his desk. Phillip stood rather stiffly near the door. "Come and sit," Mr. Morgan said while making himself comfortable behind his desk. Once Phillip was seated across from him, Mr. Morgan asked, "Are you here to discuss the lake? Your father and I had a gentleman's agreement. He granted me fishing rights, but he made it clear that when the property passed to you, I would need to renegotiate the terms."

"No, sir. I am not here about the lake. I am here to discuss the future of your daughter."

Mr. Morgan's eyebrows rose. He sat back. The jolly grin he had been sporting was now replaced with surprise. "I would hate to be presumptuous, so perhaps, you might clarify further your meaning," he said cautiously.

"You are obviously aware, I am to take over Marymoor, so I assume you suspect I am in need of a wife. I have given the matter a great deal of thought. My family has always hoped to forge an alliance with yours, and I imagine a new bride would be most content living near her parents."

Mr. Morgan was silent for several moments. He pulled his chair closer to the desk and sat straighter. "So, you are speaking of marriage? With one of my girls?"

"Yes," Phillip's throat went dry. His palms felt clammy. "You have known me all of my life, and I hope you are aware of my character and position."

Mr. Morgan's cheeks puffed out and he released a long breath. "I do not question your character. It is just that I am taken by surprise you have formed an attachment to one of my daughters so quickly."

Phillip sighed and looked away. Mr. Morgan's gaze narrowed in on him.

"You have not formed an attachment, then."

Phillip looked down into his lap. "Both of your daughters are lovely girls, sir, but no. I have not."

Nodding, Mr. Morgan said, "You have surprised me, Mr. Heartford. In my day, our parents arranged these types of unions, so I certainly have no expectations regarding attachments." He rubbed the back of his neck. "I did not have any particular attachment to my wife when we married. In fact, I hardly knew her. But now," he said, a smirk upon his face, "all the young people seem to want love matches. I do not know if such a match leads to greater happiness. After all, how can one know love without facing the trials of life together? But here you come along upsetting my notion of how the youth think. What has convinced you to take the traditional route to finding a wife?"

At long last. Phillip had prepared for this. He willed his extremities to stop shaking. "I have reached the age to marry and understand its advantages," he said. He folded his hands in his lap just in case they refused to stop twitching. "I will need a partner to manage Marymoor and produce an heir. I've grown up with your daughters. I care about them both and know they will both make excellent wives. Five years ago, Miss Morgan saved my life. She was the one who ran and found help after I broke through the ice. This is her third season, and her prospects have narrowed. The world can be harsh to a spinster."

Mr. Morgan's eyes grew wide. "Is it really her third

season?" He opened a drawer and began shuffling through papers. As he rifled, he asked, "Are you suggesting Allison has no prospects?"

"She has spurned many suitors, and this in turn has scared away others. I mention your daughter's precarious situation not to alarm you but because I want to help."

"I admit, I had thought you had Julia in mind," Mr. Morgan admitted. He pulled a stack of papers from the drawer and set them on his desk. "Do you really think Allison is in danger of not finding a match? I could increase her dowry."

"I do not know how many callers you regularly receive, Mr. Morgan. I encountered her at two balls last season, and her dance card was but half full."

Looking up briefly, Mr. Morgan asked, "Is there truly such a dearth of gentlemen?" He reached into his pocket and pulled out a pair of spectacles and dropped his head back toward the papers. "Up until now, I have left this in my wife's hands." With the spectacles in place, he scanned the documents. "It *has* been three years," he mumbled, his face growing pale.

"We can select a wedding date after the end of the season if you'd prefer. We can keep it quiet, and if she finds a better suitor, you can…"

"No. No, my boy. It is not your eligibility that concerns me. I just do not see how you can convince her. I do not think she understands how dire her circumstances are."

"If I could speak with her…"

"Yes. Of course." Mr. Morgan stood. "Could you wait in the parlor? I can show you where it is."

Phillip rose from his seat and the two men crossed the room. "There is no need to show me. I know where to find the parlor," Phillip said once they reached the door, "but, I have one request. When you send for your daughter, could you please refrain from mentioning anything about our meeting?"

A nod assured Phillip he could make his proposal on his own terms.

Standing with his back to the door, Phillip heard it open. He knew it must be her. The footsteps were too light to be her father's. He heard a gasp and swiveled to see Allison standing a few yards away. The vein in her neck stood out, and she looked so still and stiff her resemblance to a doll was striking.

"Mr. Heartford," she said, her voice was lower than normal and was devoid of emotion. "Is there something I can help you with?"

The taste of bile rose in his throat, but he swallowed and put on his best smile. He bowed. "Actually, I have a business proposition for you." He gestured toward a pair of seats. "Might we sit and discuss it?"

"I do not imagine I have a choice in that matter," Allison mumbled as she walked toward the chairs he had been eyeing. She sat down, but her back remained stiff. She positioned herself on the edge of her seat.

"It is true; women do have fewer choices in our society," he said as he took the seat opposite her. He leaned back, suggesting he was relaxed, but his knee nervously bounced. He smiled before continuing. "Which is why I think my offer may interest you. I am soon to be given my birthright—"

"I believe you mean Johnathan's birthright," Allison corrected. Her lips formed a tight line.

"Yes, indeed. That is more accurate." He sat up straighter and reached up to loosen his cravat slightly.

Reaching into a pocket hidden in the lining of his coat, he withdrew a handkerchief and used it to wipe his brow. It was an act of Providence that she had mentioned Johnathan. More than anything, he was doing this to honor his brother's memory, and in his moment of need, when he was most unsure of his plan, God had sent him a reminder to help his resolve. Allison appeared so unfeeling and cold. It was no wonder she had chased away half of London. But he had known her as a girl, and beneath this exterior she was not terrible. While they had never been close, she had always treated Johnathan kindly. "In my family, whoever is expected to take over Marymoor is expected to demonstrate he is ready for such responsibility."

Allison rolled her eyes. "And what does that have to do with me?"

He swallowed before answering. "I am expected to take a wife."

Phillip heard her sharp intake of breath. Her eyes grew wide.

"In addition to demonstrating my willingness to assume responsibility, marriage directly benefits the estate. A woman is better equipped to manage the household and a wife is more invested in running it efficiently than a housekeeper would be," he continued. He stuffed his handkerchief back into the pocket whence it came. "A wife would provide me more time to address other issues." If he looked carefully, he could see some of Julia's features in Allison's face.

"As fascinating as this is, Mr. Heartford, I do not see why this has anything to do with me."

"Well, I have political aspirations. I always have." Looking up, their eyes briefly met. He immediately looked away and shifted uncomfortably. "Being the second born, I naturally did not expect I would need to manage an estate…"

Allison's hands balled into fists and she said, "No, but

things change. And I am sure you knew you needed to adapt."

His face grew hot. "Which I am trying to do, yes. But I thought if I could find a woman who was capable of running the estate, one who enjoyed life here in Kent, I could ..."

Allison closed her eyes. "Please tell me you have come to ask for my suggestions on women who might be willing to make a lifelong commitment for a guaranteed allowance, Mr. Heartford. Otherwise, I might be forced to consider the ridiculous notion that you intend to seek a courtship with me."

Phillip was flustered. Had he truly been so ambiguous? "N-no, I do not seek a courtship or your advice," he stammered.

"Are you attempting to offer me a job?" she asked.

Was she trying to suggest alternatives to dissuade him from his purpose? It did not matter. He would not be deterred. He was persistent. If he could not win her hand today, at least there would be no confusion over his intentions. "Yes, in a way I suppose I am." His voice shook as the words fell from his lips.

Allison's eyes darted about the room. Phillip had once seen a mouse in a barn. It had scurried across the floor before noticing the large watchful eyes of an owl. In that moment, the mouse fidgeted, just as Allison did now. But unlike the mouse, Allison had determination, and he watched as her fear was replaced with resolve.

"Before you say anything further, I beg of you to explain why your family felt it was acceptable to abandon your estate for five years, yet suddenly, now that the land will be transferred to you, the estate must be managed. This reeks of hypocrisy. If your father could hold title while remaining absent, why are you expected to occupy the property?"

"It is a peculiar condition," he conceded with a sigh. "It seems that many generations ago, an heir inherited the property. He did not live on the land or learn how to manage it. Had his father not stepped in to save the estate, it might have been lost." Phillip shook his head and continued, "Not long thereafter, the man lost his wife, so the man's father again stepped in to help by offering to raise his child."

"A man unwilling to raise his own child is indeed irresponsible," Allison said.

"Yes," Phillip agreed. "Having felt as though he had failed to teach his own son the meaning of duty to his family, the old man worked to instill this quality in his ward. One such tenet that was embraced by the child was the need to bond with the land and learn to manage it." Phillip fidgeted in his seat. "Once the child grew up and assumed the responsibility for the property, he added a clause in the entitlement. Now, in order to inherit, at the time the ownership passes hands, the new family must occupy the property for five years. After that length of time, it is assumed the new owner will have a proper respect for the property and will understand what is needed to run the estate."

Allison raised an eyebrow and asked, "If the entitlement was put in place to ensure the land is well managed, your father taught you this skill before he left?"

"No." Phillip chuckled. "Ideally, he would have, but he spent his time teaching Johnathan. Entitlements are sometimes put in place with a goal in mind, but this does not guarantee the goal will be met."

The hall clock chimed the half hour and its resonant song breached the solid doors.

"If your family must live on the estate for five years, I hardly see how I can help you maintain your title to the land while you live in London."

"It is not required that my entire family live here." Phillip's knee bounced up and down rapidly. He looked in every direction but Allison's. "If I marry, my wife might live here while I live elsewhere, and the condition will be met."

"Are you suggesting that we marry so you might be able to return to London and saddle me with the responsibility of looking after your ancestral home? Further, as you do not know what you are doing, I am to accomplish this task without any sort of guidance from you?" she asked.

Phillip's eyes grew wide. He felt as if the wind had been knocked out of him. *How can she believe such a thing?* "I would say that I am offering you the freedom to live your life as you please, in a setting that you are familiar with and appreciate—which is near your family—while ensuring you have ample resources at your disposal." His words rushed forth, fueled by indignation and passion. "I am releasing you from the pressure of entertaining suitors when you have demonstrated you do not wish to marry. I am paying you the compliment of acknowledging that you are intelligent enough to run a large estate without my assistance, and I am offering you the type of security you will need upon the death of your father. Further, both of our families have long wished to see our lands united, and we would be creating this alliance. Your father is a very capable landowner, and I am sure he will be an excellent tutor."

"How dare you claim I do not wish to marry?" she asked, raising her voice. "How dare you claim to know anything about me?"

His jaw slackened, and he sputtered, "From all I have just said, that is the thing you heard?"

Her lips pursed, and she snapped, "I have heard the rest as well, sir, and am equally offended. You state I am intelligent, yet you think I am gullible enough to agree to take on the monumental task of trying to sort out an estate that has been neglected for five years because of flattery?"

"No," he uttered. He closed his eyes, hoping to make sense of this turn in the conversation. He could feel the tension in his brow. "It is security I offer."

"Ha!"

Startled, he opened his eyes and discovered her eyes lit with fury.

"If you believe I value security so much, why have I not taken one of the earlier offers that would have given me this very thing without leaving me living alone and working myself to the bone?"

Dumbfounded, Phillip could only stare. A cloud passed over the sun, causing the room to darken. This shift shook Phillip from his stupor. "I thought you unwilling to trade your freedom for security, but I offer you both. I thought with time you might have come to see the merits of my offer."

"You have jumped to conclusions about my motives because, as I stated earlier, you hardly know me. I understand you are unaware of how insulting your business proposition has been, and I acknowledge that your motives were pure, but I feel you have a habit of not thinking through the implications of your actions and you have again demonstrated this to me. I am afraid I must decline your offer, Mr. Heartford. I wish you luck in finding someone more desperate than me." Allison rose from her seat.

Phillip was shocked. He had considered that she might ask for time to contemplate his offer. He had even thought she might politely refuse, but never had he considered that she might be offended. He should have listened to Julia. She knew her sister better than anyone. Why had he allowed himself to be swayed by Caleb James?

"I hope you understand I cannot stand here all day, Mr. Heartford. I trust you know your way out?"

"Yes. Yes, of course." He stood and walked toward the

door but stopped a few feet shy. "I can see I have gone about this the wrong way, Miss Morgan. I lack experience in these matters. I do hope that should I be fortunate enough to spend time with you again in the future you will not hold my lack of knowledge against me."

"If we will speak of this no further, I will attempt to forget it ever happened."

"But if I am able to win your affection in the future, might I then renew my offer?"

"I can assure you, Mr. Heartford, such a day will never come."

Chapter Ten

"What were you thinking?" Julia paced back and forth on the lawn in front of the old barn.

"I was thinking I am considered an eligible catch. Further, I was under the impression your father approved of the match." Phillip leaned against a tree, his arms crossed over his chest.

Julia stopped marching and glared at him. "Well, it is not my father who you asked to marry you, now is it?"

"No, but my understanding is that daughters often defer to their fathers' suggestions."

Her glare intensified, making it rather obvious that she did not find his statement helpful or amusing. She took in a deep breath which she slowly released through her nose before speaking. "You have not spoken more than twenty minutes in the past five years. You cannot expect to swoop in and convince someone to marry you after so little time."

"What are you talking about?" Phillip pushed away from the tree and walked out from under its shade. "We have known each other for years. She should have a very complete picture of what sort of man I am, what life with me would entail, and if she was unaware, marriages are little more than a business agreement." Once in the sun's warm rays, he stopped and looked at Julia. He squinted his eyes and took in the fiery tempered woman before him. When she was annoyed, she hardly seemed too conscious of her plump figure—the figure he'd actually had his hands on the day before. She was a hard one to forget, with her softness, her warmth. Forcing his gaze upward, he found himself entranced by her pretty, round face, the big hazel eyes he could lose himself in, her dark hazelnut colored hair worn up and off her shoulders…and a leaf caught in the silky tresses. He caught his breath and his chest constricted as he walked toward her. Standing a little more than a foot in front of her, he freed the leaf from her hair. He then returned to his spot in the sun, again folded his arms over his chest, and said, "I come to the table with the stronger offer and uniting our two families would join our estates. This has been the wish of both families for generations. I do not understand how she could have refused."

The hard lines in Julia's face relaxed. She sighed and her shoulders sagged. "Allison wants for more than that in her marriage. She wants her marriage to be based in love."

"What a ridiculous notion."

As soon as he had spoken, he noticed how tired and resigned Julia appeared. She was a sensible woman. She must see the wisdom in his words. She too must feel the frustration and challenge of trying to counsel her foolish sister. *Do not worry, Julia, soon I will assume this responsibility.*

"You believe a love match is ridiculous? Do you not believe in love?" Julia asked. She sounded almost hurt.

Yet again, I am wrong. Julia, too, thinks her sister can find a love match. Phillip shook his head, appreciating the irony that she, of all people, should ask such a question. "When I was a young man, I once fancied myself in love. Then I learned, one sees only what one wants to see." He gave her a bittersweet smile before he schooled his expression back into one of cool indifference bordering on annoyance. "Now, I am a man, and I have put away such childish beliefs. By her own admission, she has already generated much speculation by refusing countless offers. How many more brave men can there be? Not all others possess sufficient self-confidence needed to weather being summarily rejected."

"Then you are determined to try again?" she asked. "Ask for Allison's hand, that is."

"I am." He unfolded his arms and put his hands into his pockets. "She made a foolish decision in a moment of haste. She will see reason soon enough, and I will not hold her initial reaction against her."

"That is very big of you, Mr. Heartford." Julia dropped her head until her bonnet hid her face. "If you plan to approach her again, and hope for a more favorable reaction, might I suggest you first spend some time rebuilding your friendship?"

"I expected her to come around to my point of view for practical reasons." The two stood in silence for a minute. He frowned. "Do you truly think she will be swayed by something so inconsequential as a few trips to the theater or museums?"

"I think that is exactly the type of thing that will cause her to change her mind."

"In that case, I suppose I will attempt to heed your advice." He tapped his foot rapidly. "But she is rather angry with me, and I do not imagine her agreeing to such outings. I will never claim to understand the female mind. Why should she be angry at me for making a generous offer to protect and support her throughout her life? If anyone should be angry, it should be me. She rejected my offer so swiftly it should wound my pride."

Julia sighed and shook her head. "Although I think I can convince her to at least spend time with you, I had held onto a small sliver of hope that your feelings ran deeper. I had hoped this cool response was just a façade meant to hide your pain. But if her rejection truly does not wound your pride, you are not in love, Mr. Heartford." Julia looked toward the path leading away from the barn. "Given this revelation, I do not know why I should even help you with this endeavor. I wish for more for my sister."

Phillip walked around Julia so that his body blocked her from the path, and she turned to face him. "So, it is better to die alone as a spinster rather than enter into a marriage with someone who you do not love but will treat you with respect."

"Allison will never become a spinster." Julia said the words, but the fear in her eyes suggested she did not mean them. "She is beautiful. Why she has had more offers than I can count."

"As someone not as closely associated with your family, I am privy to more gossip surrounding you." Phillip weighed in his mind the cost of proceeding in this vein. As painful as the truth might be, ignoring it would lead to greater sorrow. "She has burned many bridges and hurt the pride of several young men, some of whom have implied that it was they who chose to stop calling and that their decision was based on Allison's character flaws."

Julia's mouth hung agape. "But that is not true."

"Yet, there are several sources that have spread the lies. And, you must know that in our society, it is far easier to assume the woman is to blame if a marriage is not secured after a lengthy acquaintance than it is to blame the man."

"Do you mean to say no one will take her?" Tears pooled in the corners of Julia's eyes. "Is that why you have come to make your offer?"

He nodded slowly. "In part," he said. "I also need a wife and she will do as well as the next. And, if she marries, I think you will find more opportunities will present themselves to you."

Julia looked shaken. He longed to reach out and comfort her. "Please, do not concern yourself on my account. If a man avoids me because they believe false rumors about my sister, I hardly think they are worthy of my time. But you have caused me concern on my sister's behalf." She turned and resumed her pacing. "If her future looks so bleak, I must help you." She'd said the words out loud, but she had spoken so softly it was as though she was attempting to convince herself. Before continuing, she looked straight into Phillip's eyes. With urgency in her voice she said, "But you must not act so boldly again. Allison wants and deserves love. Yes, she may be selfish at times, but she is so much more than that. You must woo her. I think I can convince her to spend time with you, but you must only try to gain her friendship at first."

Despite his best effort to hide his feelings, his eyes widened in surprise, but after a moment he regained control, pushing a false smile over his features and jutting out his jaw. "Until I was rejected so soundly, I was unaware I did not already possess her friendship," he said, reaching up and smoothing his cravat.

"Truly?" Julia blinked in surprise. "After your last interaction, when you called upon us, this was unclear to you?"

Phillip turned away from Julia and watched a pair of birds dancing midair. "I thought that we just had preferred bantering with each other," he said quietly. "I did not view it as arguing."

She tried to stifle her laugh with a cough. "Well," she said after clearing her throat, "I think you would find she has a different perspective on that matter. Believe me, you need to earn her friendship. If I agree to help you, you must wait until I tell you before attempting to again progress the relationship further."

Phillip elevated his right eyebrow. He turned back and looked Julia in the eye. "Are you suggesting I try to win her heart?"

"No. I do not think you are looking for love, and it

would be very unfair for you to make her love you when you will not reciprocate. I am hoping that you will be able to make her fond enough of you that she can weigh what you are offering against her other options without allowing her emotions to impact her reasoning." A breeze blew across the field, and Julia hugged her arms.

"Do you think that will be sufficient to get her to say yes?"

She pulled her shawl tightly around her shoulders. "I do not know, but I think it is important that you both are able to logically consider your options."

"I have managed to secure an invitation to tour the hothouse. Would that be too soon to attempt to forge this friendship, or should I plan on meeting you there?"

Julia stood for a moment in silence, her lips forming an asymmetrical purse. "You say that she indicated she would pretend this never happened?" she asked.

"Actually, I think she said she would *forget* it ever happened."

"Then yes, come to the tour, but do not come to call before then. I will speak with her and attempt to soften her, so she is more receptive to seeing your charms."

Chapter Eleven

The carriage carrying the Morgan girls rolled along at a leisurely pace. There was no practical reason for the languid speed. It was just one of those days where everyone relaxes and the whole world slows down. Perhaps, the horses wanted to enjoy their surroundings, or the driver had allowed his mind to drift. One could not pinpoint the cause, but even Mother Nature showed her lethargic tendencies finding it easier to hold her breath than to breathe. And when she did release a small puff of air, it was so weak it barely caused a flutter in even the lightest of tree branches. Both sisters were content to forgo conversation in exchange for the comfort of relative silence. The sounds of the carriage, the birds, and the clopping of horses was sufficient entertainment for the short jaunt to the Everlys' estate. It was for these reasons it came as a small shock to Julia when her sister addressed her.

"Julia, I know that you have no particular interest in horticulture, so I want to thank you for accompanying me," Allison said while reaching over and taking Julia's hand in her own. "It has been a trying week, and the prospect of this outing with you has managed to make it bearable."

A wave of guilt washed over Julia. "Was it that business with Mr. Heartford that you found distressing?"

"Yes, in a way. Had it simply been his proposal alone, I might have been able to ignore it, but Papa's endless badgering was just too much." Allison gave Julia's hands a squeeze before releasing them and settling back into her seat. A warm smile settled over her face. "But today, I do not want to even think about that man. Today, it will just be you, me, and Miss James."

The coach rolled through the gates of the Everlys' estate, and both girls stared out the windows. Allison wore an expression of awe and excitement Julia noted with a frown. The driver had been instructed to take the coach to the back of the house as it was closer to the gardens and would make the most efficient use of their time. As the carriage rounded the house, Miss James came into view. Her brother stood next to her and hurrying across the field to join them was Phillip Heartford.

Allison's gaze turned toward her sister. The warmth and affection that had filled her eyes moments before was gone, only to be replaced by the fire of anger that lingered in their place.

"Were you aware he would be joining us?" Allison hissed as the carriage pulled to a stop.

"How can any of us know what actions another will take?" Julia asked with a nervous smile.

Caleb waved off the footman and stepped forward. After opening the door, he extended his hand to Allison and greeted her. "Miss Morgan. How nice to see you again." Once Allison was securely on firm ground, he assisted and greeted Julia in much the same manner.

Violet James rushed forth and took a hand of each girl. "I am so happy you could make it. I hope you do not mind, but my brother and his friend will be joining us."

The Morgan sisters nodded to Phillip, who had successfully joined the group, and he bowed in return.

Miss James linked arms with Allison and led the group toward the hothouse. "I do not think we could have asked for a finer day," she said cheerfully.

Phillip offered his arm to Julia, and they trailed behind Miss James and Allison. Caleb lingered in the back. A sufficient amount of space existed between the three sets that it was not possible to speak as a group. Such substantial intervals did, however, ensure private conversations could be had, a quality Julia took full advantage of.

Leaning in closely, Julia said, "I have done my utmost to persuade my sister to forgive your faux pas, Mr. Heartford, but my father refused to let the topic drop. It has caused a great deal of tension in our home, and whether it is merited or not, Allison holds you partially responsible."

The muscles on Phillip's neck twitched. "I was just about to mention that I've missed your friendship these past few days, but if you choose to categorize my proposal as a faux pas, I might need to reconsider," he said before stuffing his hands into his pockets. "If anything, it was the manner in which I was refused that demonstrates a lack of etiquette."

"Oh. For heaven's sake." Julia took her hand from his arm and playfully swatted him. "Do you still wish to marry her or not?"

"Yes, but I will not have my manners criticized when I have done nothing wrong." He lifted his chin and folded his arms across his chest. "If anything, I was acting nobly."

Julia sighed. "My mistake. I did not intend to imply otherwise. It was merely a poor choice of words." She reached up and placed her hand on his forearm. She hoped the action acted as a reminder that he was meant to be escorting her. He dropped his arm. "Thank you," she said once they had resumed their prior poses. Her hand felt as if it was meant to be here, as if Phillip's arm was home. *Perhaps he is right. Perhaps he is meant to be my brother.*

After a few paces, she noticed the silence. "I had only meant to say that my sister feels pressure from our father, and she has transferred any stress this has caused onto you. If she is a bit—difficult, do not take it personally."

With a small smirk, Phillip leaned in and whispered, "I would expect no less from her and never do take it personally. However, it has been my experience that she will avoid me until I am forgiven."

Julia pressed her index finger to her lips. After a moment's reflection, she said, "When the opportunity arises, I will make an excuse to draw Mr. and Miss James away from her. You must use that time to ingratiate yourself. You have much ground to recover."

"I will do my best. It is a pity your sister does not have your amiable nature," he replied.

They walked a few feet in silence before Julia asked, "Did you really miss me?"

"I did." He looked away, causing her to be disappointed that she could no longer see his face. "I actually picked you up something from town. The next time we are alone I will give it to you."

Julia raised her hand to her mouth. "You did not get me a gift! That would be scandalous."

"Do not consider it a gift. Consider it a small thank you for all of your assistance."

Phillip had to concentrate to refrain from moaning once they entered the greenhouse. The room was heavy with the scent of flowers, which he found nauseating. While he did not dislike plants, he was not overly fond of the dirt and insects that so frequently accompanied greenery. He silently prayed that Miss James believed in the idea of brevity when giving tours.

"My great aunt had an interest in horticulture and had this structure built in 1779," Violet began. In an instant, Phillip understood his prayers would remain unanswered. "Her husband then began presenting her with exotic plants from around the world." She led the group down a pathway through the well-organized conservatory. They came to a stop in front of a door that appeared to lead to a small room which was walled off from the rest of the area. "My great uncle gifted her plants from the Americas. Many of these varieties thrive under conditions that are far warmer and drier than those here in England. He had this area cordoned off in order to create an environment that is more in keeping with these plants' native habitat." Violet paused and looked to her brother.

He had not followed her down the path. Rather, he had remained near the entrance several yards away. He looked content with his back resting against the doorframe, his legs crossed, and arms folded.

"Caleb, come closer," Violet called. "You can't see anything from there."

He uncrossed his legs and placed one foot against the door frame. "I am not here to view the plants. I have seen them before," he replied lazily. "I would rather stay out of the way and allow our guests to enjoy them. I can see all I need to from here."

Phillip looked wistfully toward the door and felt the pangs of envy.

Violet shrugged. "As you wish." She turned to the three guests who were in her immediate vicinity. "The area behind this door is fairly small, it might be best if I take you in one at a time."

When it was at last Julia's turn to accompany Miss James into the small room to see the sedum, Allison surprised both men by asking Phillip to accompany her to the opposite corner of the room to admire the citrus trees.

They stopped in front of a small group of trees that were in bloom. Allison sighed and shook her head. "Well, that could not have worked out better for the lot of you," she said.

"Pardon?" Phillip asked, his surprise and confusion reflected in his voice.

"You are not here because of your interest in plants, Mr. Heartford. You came today to convince me of the error of my ways. To do this, you needed to find some way to speak to me, and now, no one will be required to create some silly excuse in an effort to give us an opportunity to be alone," she replied, as if her meaning should have been perfectly clear. "Surely, you cannot think I am so naïve to not see what you are attempting to do."

Phillip crossed his arms and jutted out his jaw in a show of defiance. "Miss Morgan, your assessment may be accurate, but all the same, one would not normally point it out so directly."

"I am nothing if not direct," she responded. If she was bothered by Phillip's sulking, she gave no indication. Instead, she said, "I am going to ask you a simple question, and I'd appreciate an honest answer. Why have you returned to Marymoor?" She fixed her gaze on him carefully.

Phillip shifted uncomfortably, feeling as though she were searching every line of his face, scrutinizing even the most minute of movements. He tried to hide his annoyance and vowed to himself to consider strategies that could help him accommodate her quirks after they were married. "If my declaration was not obvious enough, I have come home to win your favor in the hopes that this will allow me to win your hand," he answered.

She snorted. "And why do you seek my hand?" she pressed.

Phillip closed his eyes and reached up and rubbed his temples. With the passion of a turnip he replied, "Why does any suitor pursue such a thing? Love, of course."

Her eyes sparkled with mirth and her laughter filled the air. "Your lie is so blatant you cannot even convince yourself."

"Was that not what you wanted to hear?"

"What I want is for you to be honest—not only with me but also with yourself." Allison rolled her eyes and looked away from him.

The trees in front of them were still young. They might bloom, but they were not ready to fruit.

"You are not an unpleasant man, Mr. Heartford..."

"Very glad to hear it," he chimed in.

"But," she said giving him a look that silenced him, "we are not suited to each other. In time, I imagine we could learn to like each other, but you can never rewrite history and convince me it is fact. We did not get along as children. You would not have returned here because you had love in your heart. At least not love for me."

Phillip smirked. "I have heard, Miss Morgan, that boys in their misguided attempts to show affection, often show their love in awkward and ineffective ways." He plucked a bloom from the tree and offered it to her.

Allison looked over her shoulder and Phillip followed her gaze. The door to the area where Julia was remained closed, and Mr. James was staring at a spot on the floor as if it were the most fascinating thing he'd ever seen. "A very valiant effort," she hissed, "but I am not as trusting as my sister. And if you insist on pursuing this, Mr. Heartford, I will discover the true reason you are here."

"And I wish to discover what one must do to gain your agreement to a courtship, Miss Morgan." His eyes fixed on the closed door.

A movement caught his attention and Phillip glanced over to Caleb. Caleb had rocked away from the doorframe. Standing erect, with his arms crossed over his chest, he cleared his throat. Phillip immediately understood the significance of the glance being cast in his direction. He turned back to Allison. "They are nearly done, Miss Morgan. Perhaps we should move to the other end of the room."

She nodded, and the two crossed the space in an uncomfortable silence.

"How was your outing?" Mrs. Morgan asked. She was sitting at her secretary writing when her daughters returned.

"I saw some plants from the Americas I had not yet seen," Allison said.

Mrs. Morgan frowned as she rose to her feet and crossed the room. "You seem less enthusiastic than I would have expected." She took Allison's chin in her hand, lifted her face, and studied it. "You are not growing ill I hope."

"No, Mama. I am just tired."

Dropping her hand to her side, Mrs. Morgan said, "What a shame. I know how much you were looking forward to this outing. Why don't you run along and get some rest before dinner?"

Obviously, the prospect of having some time to be alone appealed greatly to Allison, for she required no additional prompting to retreat to her room. Once she was gone, Mrs. Morgan turned to Julia.

"And did you enjoy the trip, my dear?" she nonchalantly asked her youngest.

"Oh, yes. I cannot say I found the plants very interesting, but the company was lovely. Mr. James and Mr.

Heartford joined us."

"Did they?" Mrs. Morgan looked to the letter she had been writing. "I was just writing to Anne. I know that I told you I was going to allow you to stay here a little longer, but given that I was mistaken about where Mr. Heartford's affection lay, I see no reason to keep you here."

Julia's shoulders dropped. "You're sending me to London?" A bout of light headedness assaulted her, and her stomach flip-flopped.

"Do not fear," her mother said returning to her letter. "I will send your sister along, and she will help you."

"But doesn't she need to stay here…I mean, with Mr. Heartford at Marymoor…"

Mrs. Morgan waved her hand, brushing away the conversation. "I do not think she particularly cares for the man," she said. "Your father may be convinced that her options are limited, but I know my daughter. When she finds something she wants, she will ultimately get it. And I see no reason to force her to waste time here when there is nothing in Kent that she is interested in."

Her mother picked up her quill and resumed writing.

Julia remained standing.

Without looking up from her letter, Mrs. Morgan asked, "Is there something you need?"

"I was just thinking that if I stayed home…"

Mrs. Morgan set down her quill and spun around in her chair so quickly it made Julia jump. "For goodness sakes! Sometimes the only way to gain something you need is to get away from it," her mother snapped. "Now go practice your piano."

Julia walked away. *Perhaps Mama is right. If I leave home and prove to Papa that I will not be able to find a husband, he may at last agree to allow me to start my own home.*

Chapter Twelve

Allison looked across the carriage. Sitting with her fist to her mouth and staring out the window, sat Julia. Her brow was creased, and Allison would have bet money that there was an enormous frown hiding under that fist. "Why do you look so glum?" she asked.

"Need you ask?" Julia did not bother to look at her sister. "You know how I have been dreading this." She tried to soak in the last of the countryside—the trees, the fields, the clear, blue sky. Once she arrived at aunt's house, all she would see when she looked out the window would be towering buildings and smoke. At least Allison would be close. They usually shared a room while visiting London.

Allison rolled her eyes. "If the prospect of attending the season distresses you so, why did you not refuse?"

"I did go to Papa. I told him there was no need for me to attend the season. I told him that I wished to use my inheritance to live a modest, comfortable life, and for this I did not require a husband. He told me that there is a stark difference between possessing funds and accessing them."

"He knows your downfall," Allison said. She dropped her head back down and opened a book. "You do not believe in yourself enough."

"Cedrick, do you think the blue or the gold looks best?"

Phillip studied the two waistcoats he held out.

"I prefer the green, sir."

Phillip turned to the green silk he had tossed on a nearby chair. Prissy, the cat he had acquired on the day he was invited to the garden party, lay curled up on it. There was no need to wake her to know that the green waistcoat would now be covered in hair. He did not know Allison's preference, but Julia preferred blue. "I think I will go with the blue," he said. He had tried all week to convince himself that he had chased the Morgan girls to London because of Allison. This was his duty, and he was simply dedicated to fulfilling it. But when he had called on their family and discovered they had left Kent, it was not thoughts of Allison that had flooded his mind. No. It had been the idea that Julia was no longer near that had caused fear and panic to course through his veins. Of course, that was simply because he needed to protect her, as a brother should. If she was not near, he could not keep her safe. It was nothing more than that. Allison was shrewd. She did not need someone to keep an eye on her.

"Cedrick, you are certain you heard Mr. James correctly?"

"Yes, sir. He asked that I tell you the Morgan sisters would be there tonight."

Once Cedrick had finished dressing him, Phillip flew down the stairs. His carriage was waiting, for his indecision had delayed his departure. As the carriage came to a stop in front of the Weston's mansion, Phillip closed his pocket watch and put it away. The festivities had started ten minutes earlier.

He exited his carriage but did not make it far before he encountered his friend Fitz. The two greeted each other warmly.

"Why are you not already inside?" Phillip asked.

With a shrug, Fitz replied, "I served my time and

greeted those most likely to report my appearance to my father. Now, I can go play cards." He looked at Phillip a moment before asking, "Care to join me? It is late in the season. Surely, you must have had your fill of these things by now."

Phillip shook his head. "Not tonight, I'm afraid."

The friends said goodbye and Phillip climbed the stairs two at a time. As he approached the front door, he stopped to greet Mr. and Mrs. Green, friends of his parents.

"Mr. Heartford," Mrs. Green said gleefully, "I am so pleased to see you again. We ran into your parents in Cromwell, and your mother could not stop telling us about your accomplishments."

Phillip's cheeks grew warm. He did not know if it was the exertion of climbing the stairs so quickly or the compliment. "My mother is not terribly objective," he replied.

"No. None of us are, really." She leaned in, and her smile faded. "But I watched her recover from the shock of Johnathan's death. He was very dear to her, you know. Without you, I do not know that she could have survived."

Phillip swallowed a lump in his throat. For five years, Johnathan had plagued him. Every day Johnathan had guided him in his actions. But when he had discovered Julia was gone, he had forgotten to think about his brother. Now, hearing Mrs. Green's words, it was as if the ghost had reappeared. "We all miss him greatly."

"He too would have been so proud of you. You seem to be achieving all of his goals."

"He did give his life to save mine," Phillip said before clearing his throat. "The least I can do is try to live enough for the both of us."

Mrs. Green's kind smile returned. "What a lovely way to honor him. I am sure he is watching down on you now, grateful you are doing so much to pay tribute to him."

Mr. Green touched his wife's hand. "It was wonderful to see you, Heartford, but we should be going in now. Lilian is going to play tonight."

After checking their coats and hats, the three entered the main hall. While the Greens took their seats, Phillip scanned the crowd. His eyes immediately fell on Julia and Allison. They stood near the punch bowl, laughing. He took a step forward before seeing the young man who had at first been obscured behind Allison. His pace quickened.

"Miss Morgan, Miss Julia," he greeted, the entire time his eyes fixed on this stranger.

"Oh, Mr. Heartford, what a surprise. I hadn't known you had returned to London," Allison said. She was exuding charm, which took Phillip by surprise.

"Well, it seems our entire town has fled to the city. I could not allow myself to be left behind."

With one of her signature smiles, Allison replied, "Indeed, not. I was hoping, Mr. Heartford, that you could accompany me. I forgot to collect a program."

Phillip offered Allison his arm, and they walked away from the punch bowl. It took every ounce of control he possessed to resist turning back to look at Julia. He was leaving her alone with a man he knew nothing about. Images assaulted his mind: her alabaster skin against her dark ruby dress, the fabric that gracefully fell over her body revealing each of her curves, the silky tendrils of hair that had escaped her coiffeur and drew the eye to her collar bone. The sound of her laughter seemed to echo in the room. Surely, even a fairy nymph could not produce a more enticing sound. She would tempt any man, and he did not care for the way that man in particular had been looking at her. Why, now of all times, had Allison become so interested in his company? He had only chosen Allison so he could protect Julia, but how was he to do that from across the room?

The rest of the evening proved to be equally frustrating. When he tried to speak to Julia, Allison intervened. Every time Julia managed to free herself from the piranhas, her sister would find another to throw in her path. Allison, who when not avoiding him had, until now, always been aloof, suddenly found him fascinating and acted almost clingy. He had counted her independence among her attributes, and this new facet of her personality left him greatly concerned for their future. The entire evening was infuriating. He had to escape, and after an hour, he found an opportunity.

Upon returning home, he took a bath and settled into his library. A good book generally proved to be an excellent distraction. Tonight, however, even his favorite tome had lost its allure. He looked to the chair on his right. Prissy was perched on an arm rest, and her bright green eyes stared up at him. He reached out and stroked her behind her ears. She rewarded him with a purr.

Phillip took a deep breath and leaned back in his own seat. "What shall I do?" he asked the cat.

With a swish of her tale, Prissy hopped from her seat and walked away.

All women are a mystery, regardless of the species. Phillip closed his book. No sooner had he stood to place it back on the shelf than Cedrick entered, carrying a calling card.

"Who can possibly be calling at this hour?" Phillip asked even as he removed the card from the tray. The question was rhetorical for there was only one answer and a quick peek at the card confirmed the obvious. "Tell Mr. James I am in my banyan and am not receiving visitors."

The door opened and Caleb strolled in. He turned to Cedrick. "Tell Mr. Heartford I have now seen him in his banyan, and if I am forced to listen to Lilian Green perform and attend an event that he does not even have the decency to stay at, he will see me."

Cedrick looked to his employer and Phillip waved him away. He left without a word. Prissy too slipped out through the door before it was closed. *Avoiding Mr. James, I see. That cat is an excellent judge of character.*

"You have the manners of a sea urchin," Phillip said, pulling his robe around himself tightly. "If you insist on visiting, allow me to change."

"Will you return, or is it your intention to run away given that this might be perceived as a social call?"

Phillip glared at him but left without a response. When he returned, fully dressed, Caleb was not in the library. Phillip went to his study and found Mr. James sitting in a chair, smoking one of the cigars he kept in a locked drawer. Before he could ask how his guest had gained access to his drawer, Caleb spoke.

"Where were you?"

"What? Getting dressed." Phillip had to wonder at times why he remained friends with this man.

"No. Tonight. Where were you?"

"Do you mean the event?"

Caleb nodded.

"Not that it is any of your concern, but when I arrived, I did not feel well, so I left after the first few performances," Phillip answered. He walked over to the drawer, unlocked it, and removed a cigar for himself. "How did you get into my cigars?"

"Fitz told me where you hide the key," Caleb said with the same amount of indifference he might use to give someone directions. "I was there specifically to support you and assist you in winning the affections of your young lady. And you felt unwell?" This was said with more of an accusatory tone. An eyebrow was raised, and he watched Phillip with such scrutiny, Phillip felt physically uncomfortable.

"You barge into my house, steal my cigars, and have the audacity to interrogate me in the middle of the night—"

"Yes. And it is a single cigar."

Phillip sank into a chair. He snipped off the end of his cigar, but before lighting it, he tossed it on his desk. It had been a trying night. His head fell into his hands and he rubbed his temples. Wearily he looked at Caleb who showed no trace of his typical carefree attitude. Phillip needed someone to talk to, and, as always, Caleb had known. After releasing a deep breath, Phillip said, "I... I do not know if I can do this."

"Do what? Reliably attend and participate in a social event?"

Phillip rolled his eyes. "No. I do not know if I can marry Miss Morgan."

Caleb took a few puffs before responding. "Well, as she does not appear to be prepared to marry you either, I do not see the reason for the long face." He reached over and grabbed an ashtray. With a flick of his wrist, he knocked the ash from the tip of his cigar. "There is something else. Why do you not know if you can marry her?"

"Because a man always wants what he cannot have," Phillip said, more to himself. If only he hadn't run into Mrs. Green. He had started to believe he might be able to allow himself to be happy and having that sliver of hope before falling into darkness was so much worse than having never seen the light.

Chapter Thirteen

It was only after a significant amount of prodding that Phillip found himself calling on the Morgan daughters the following morning. He quickly discovered that Allison had returned to her usual self, largely ignoring him. He had little doubt that had her aunt not been present, she would have treated him far worse. But he was finally afforded the opportunity to speak with Julia, and that soothed his heart like nothing else could have.

"I am terribly sorry we were unable to speak last night, Mr. Heartford. Allison has so many acquaintances. I had no idea how busy I would be kept." Julia glowed this morning. Phillip wondered if her confidence had been bolstered by the attention she had received the previous evening. She hummed while arranging the flowers he had brought in a vase.

"Leave those alone," her aunt called across the room. "We can let the servants take care of that."

Julia glanced over at her aunt and, seeing that she had refocused her attention on her needlepoint, moved two of the roses to the front of the vase. Gently she plucked some leaves away from the greenery, allowing the colors of the flowers an unobstructed view of the room. She bent over and inhaled the sweet fragrance of a bloom before removing a thorn from its stem. Phillip was mesmerized. She was graceful and elegant.

An image danced through his mind of her arranging the centerpiece in the grand foyer at Marymoor. Her earrings would catch the light from the window, just as it had when his mother would perform this task. She would make a wonderful mistress, he thought. This would not do. He could not simply stand here, staring at her. "Are you enjoying London, Miss Julia?" he asked, hoping to sweep these images away.

"I find it overwhelming. But it is so nice to see a familiar face. Thank you for visiting."

Phillip offered her his arm, and together they returned to the side of the room where her aunt sat. "I was actually very disappointed to discover you had left Kent. I thought if you intended to leave, you might have mentioned it to me."

"Our mother made the decision rather suddenly," Julia explained. They were still several yards from the couch where her aunt sat. Julia stopped. She leaned in and asked, "You were really disappointed to find I had left?"

"Yes." He looked up and saw Allison glaring in his direction. "And Miss Morgan too, of course."

Julia frowned. "Right. I should have mentioned she would be leaving. It would be difficult to win her affections from afar." Though she had spoken out loud, she appeared to be speaking to herself. She added with a weak smile, "You seemed to be getting along quite well last night."

"It has always been easier with you. With that one, we are back to square one." Through a nearly imperceptible nod of his head he motioned to Allison.

Julia looked over. Her hand flew to her mouth hiding a laugh. "By the look on her face, I think you are fortunate she is not armed, Mr. Heartford. While it is entirely implausible in her case, I would almost guess she is jealous."

"That is not a look of jealousy. That is a look that a mother bear gives a hunter when she is protecting her cubs."

"Do you think she believes you dangerous?"

"I cannot say. I have known your sister long enough to feel I can predict her behaviors with some accuracy, but I have never been able to guess her thoughts."

"What is keeping you two?" Julia's aunt called. She patted the seat cushion next to her.

The two resumed walking. "If you are free this afternoon at two, Mr. Weston has asked us to join him for a walk in Hyde Park, near the area where the entrance to the Great Fair had been. Should you happen to be there, you could join us. It might enable you to ask Allison what she is thinking."

"Is Mr. Weston that charming young man you were speaking to near the punch bowl?"

"Yes. Allison has a silly notion about him and me," she explained.

"I will see you at two."

"What are you two whispering about?" Allison asked.

"Nothing of consequence," Julia replied. They picked up their pace and joined the rest of the family.

Although no reward was necessary to entice Phillip to join Julia's party at Hyde Park that afternoon, the looks on the faces of Allison and Mr. Weston when he appeared provided him so much amusement that he felt handsomely rewarded. At first, Allison looked livid. But if his assessment of her feelings was accurate, she artfully masked her true feelings within seconds. Then, before he knew it, she had claimed his arm, slowed their pace, and had again isolated him from Julia.

Once they were out of earshot, Allison leaned into him and asked, "What are you up to, Mr. Heartford?"

"As I said, I was out walking and just happened to see your party."

Allison pursed her lips. A vein on the side of her neck

pulsed. After a few tense minutes of silence, she said, "Years ago, I had an experience that taught me things are rarely as you believe them to be. Since your return, I have debated with myself over divulging the specifics of that lesson to you."

"I would appreciate any lesson you would care to impart, Miss Morgan. As you know, I think there are advantages to a match between us." He reached up and loosened his cravat. "However, I am aware that our relationship has been strained since my return. You have stated we were not close as children, but we were at least considerate and congenial. I cannot account for the shift, but I think if we can return our relationship to its former status, we could find contentment in marriage."

Allison took a deep breath, and her hand dropped from his arm. "I was there the day Johnathan died," she said.

"Yes," he said. Without missing a step, he swooped down and picked up a flower that had blown off a tree and landed on the path. He turned to her with both eyebrows raised and one palm facing up. "I know. You ran and retrieved help."

"No," she said more insistently, "I was in the woods *before* you walked onto the lake. I heard what you said to each other, before… before he died."

For a second, Phillip thought his heart had stopped. He dropped the flower. Then he attempted to resume his look of indifference. "I'm sorry," he said lifting one shoulder. "I'm afraid I do not remember anything before the accident."

Allison's eyes narrowed. "Really? I believe you do." Phillip refused to look in her direction. "You argued. You had seen Julia in Johnathan's arms. You were confronting him about it. He told you that you had no claim on her. He said they were in love. It was perfectly obvious you felt the pain of a scorned lover."

A wave of disorientation washed over him. The sounds

99

surrounding him appeared to fade. He imagined he could hear the beating of his own heart, but perhaps, he was merely able to feel it pounding. His mouth was dry, but in a shaky voice that was barely audible he uttered, "You heard that? I... I was so angry at him... at them both really." He began to tremble, and his eyes stung. "He told me not to go out on the lake. He told me the ice was thinning. But I needed to get away from him— to be alone. I wanted to go somewhere where he wouldn't follow me." He stopped walking. His head fell and he held the bridge of his nose. "He was always afraid of the lake. I did not know it had thawed so much. I had been on it a few days before." He took comfort knowing Mr. Weston and Julia were engrossed in conversation and were unlikely to look back at them. Allison gave him a comforting pat on the arm. "It's my fault," he choked out the words. He reached into a pocket and withdrew his handkerchief. He took a deep breath and tried to rein in his emotions.

"No," Allison said firmly. "I know how it feels to hold onto guilt for years. To ask yourself if you had done something differently, if you had said something else. I know what it is like to need to have a reason. To need someone to blame." She blinked away her tears, "But his death was a senseless tragedy. I accept that now, and I advise you to do likewise."

They stood in silence, each in their own world. Phillip was the first to return to the present. "Thank you," he said softly.

She gave him a nod. Once the moment had passed, they resumed the walk.

Allison blurted out, "Have you come back for Julia? If you have not, I will not permit you to interfere with her efforts to find a husband."

He looked at her, his eyebrows knitted together. "No. Johnathan won her heart. How could I take more from him?"

He reached out to take her hand, but she artfully dodged his maneuvers. "I meant it when I said I wish for your hand," he pleaded. "My parents had always hoped their eldest would unite with the Morgans. I admit, in my youth I harbored silly notions of being in love with Julia, but it was only because I misunderstood her kindness as affection. I have grown up and am no longer that foolish boy. Perhaps, describing my feelings for you as love is hyperbole, but I do have affection and," he offered her a weak smile, "I know we can learn to make each other happy."

He offered his arm, and she placed a hand on his sleeve. "As romantic as this confession has been," she said with a smile, "there is a secret I have been keeping from you. I believe it has caused you no small measure of suffering, and I am sorry for withholding this information." She released a breath and leaned toward him. "I loved Johnathan, and I was jealous when I heard him confess to you in the woods. I was angry with Julia for making him fall in love with her."

"I, better than any other, understand. You do not need to explain or apologize…."

"No," she cut him off. Annoyance and impatience oozed from her pores. "You did not let me finish. Julia never loved Johnathan. He was lying to you. He only said it because he knew, as well as I did, that she only ever wanted you. He told you they were in love to keep you away from her, hoping that if you weren't there, he could win her heart."

Phillip shook his head. "But I saw them together…"

"What you saw," she interrupted, "was Johnathan catching her after she had tripped on a tree root." She removed her hand from his sleeve and clasped her hands together. "Julia had been mortified. She came home crying a few days before your confrontation and told me all about it. She was worried she had put herself in a compromising position, but I assured her no one had witnessed the aftermath of her accident. That was why I was there that day. I followed Johnathan into the woods. I wanted to make sure her reputation would remain unharmed."

Phillip again stopped walking. His arms dropped to his sides and he mumbled to himself, "But I stopped him first."

"Yes. I knew I had taken a risk following him to such a secluded location, and I thought I would wait until you passed before making my presence known." Allison bit the edge of her lip. "But then he fell in and all I could think of was to get help. After he died... I thought of telling you. But I blamed you for his death, and I was angry with Julia for capturing his heart." She took a few paces, turned, and walked back. A tear rolled down her cheek. She looked at Phillip. Her eyes filled with remorse. "I felt robbed of my happiness, and I was angry. I acted out of vengeance. I let you believe she was in love with him. And when you were recovering, when she begged to see you, I let her wonder why she was refused admission."

Phillip stared at the ground for several seconds. He swallowed. Finally, he said with a wobble in his voice, "Thank you for telling me all this, but I do not see how this changes anything."

Much like the day's mood swiftly shifts when a cloud passes over the sun, Allison's remorse and regret was replaced with anger and incredulity. "She is still in love with you. And—I have seen how your face lights up when you are near her. You love her as well. But if you intend to toy with her emotions, I will make you suffer just as Johnathan would have."

Phillip's eyes snapped up. "You have given me much to think about, Miss Morgan. Once we catch up with the others, I hope you will excuse me."

"They are not far ahead. You may go. I will make your

excuses."

Chapter Fourteen

Caleb sat with one leg over his knee and his fingers steepled. A fire raged behind him. Peering over the tips of his fingers, his eyes were trained on Phillip, who paced back and forth. "Do stop that," he snapped. "You are making me dizzy." He waved Phillip over. "Sit down before you wear a hole through the rug."

Phillip trudged toward the fire. He looked at the empty chair before collapsing into it. As soon as his legs touched the seat, his knee began to bounce.

Caleb groaned. "You are like a puppy dog. You have far too much energy."

"I'm nervous," Phillip said.

Drumming the tips of his fingers together, Caleb asked, "Are you sure it is not excitement?"

"No! Why would I be excited? I came here to marry Miss Morgan. Not only does she refuse to consider my offer, she has made an outrageous claim, and I no longer know how to act toward Miss Julia."

"Imagine that," Caleb said with amusement dancing across his features. "A girl rejects your offer because you are in love with her younger sister."

Phillip snapped his head up and glared at Caleb. "I never said I was in love with her." He ran his hands through his hair and moaned. "Yes, when I was young and immature, I may have believed that to be the case, but now..." He paused. *What do I feel toward her?* "She and I are meant to be brother and sister."

Caleb lowered his hands to his lap and cocked his head to one side. "You can tell yourself something one hundred times, but it will not make it so. I have watched you together." He wore a smirk. "I can assure you, you looked far more comfortable and intimate together than I have ever looked when I am with Violet." Caleb picked up a drink from the table beside his chair and took a sip. He swirled the glass and watched the liquid form a small funnel. He did not look up when he spoke. "Let me ask you something. Fitz is the son of a duke. He is the kind of eligible, young bachelor mercenary matchmakers salivate over. Since you have such a strong brotherly affection for Miss Julia, I imagine you would be overjoyed if I ask my mother to throw a little dinner party, and I made sure our friend was paired with your younger sister."

Phillip's eyes grew wide. He sprung from his chair and again began pacing. "Why would you do such a thing? She is not at all his type."

With wide-eyed innocence, Caleb looked up from his seat and asked, "Is that what bothers you? I could ask Fitz to bring along one of his friends. Did you know he has started a new habit of bringing along a bachelor to all of the social events he attends? He feels it is wise to carry a sacrifice for the mercenaries should they get too close and attempt to rob him of his freedom. I am sure he can bring a quality one that would find Miss Julia simply charming."

"No. That is quite enough. Miss Julia has only just come out of the school room. It would be bad form for any gentleman to show an interest in her. Especially, while her elder sister is still out and unattached."

"How peculiar. Maybe someone should mention that to—was it Mr. Weston?" Caleb stood and walked over to a cabinet.

"Her sister is behind that ridiculous attempt at a match. I am certain her parents would prefer to have the elder one engaged before thrusting bachelors in Miss Julia's direction."

"Yet, they have sent Miss Julia here to London?"

"Not to find a husband," Phillip snapped. Caleb's words had given Phillip a heavy sinking feeling in the pit of his stomach. *Surely, she is not expected to accept a proposal this season.* "She is simply attending this season to gain experience," Phillip said, with a confidence he did not feel. "Her father knows my intentions toward Miss Morgan and will wait until our engagement is official before Julia is to seriously consider suitors. This year, her presence in London is only meant to help her overcome her insecurity and to give her exposure. Next year, she will come out in earnest."

"Humm, exposure." Caleb pulled out a decanter and refilled his glass. "Then I do not see the harm in introducing her to a few of my friends. Did you not say you were looking to marry Miss Morgan to ensure Miss Julia would find success? Added exposure, as you say, will help prepare her."

Phillip narrowed his eyes and glared at his host under hooded lids. "What you suggest is premature."

Caleb crossed the room with his signature style of smooth elegance. "And when the months pass and she is dancing with a string of men, you will feel nothing but happiness at her success?"

Phillip's face grew heated. "At this moment, I can think of no suitors that are good enough."

"Of course, you cannot." Caleb leaned back in his chair and put his feet up on a nearby ottoman. "Because you are in love with her."

"I am." The words had poured forth on their own, but as his ears heard them, Phillip had no doubt of their veracity. "But she is not in love with me," he added as an afterthought.

Phillip returned to the seat near the fire, flopped down, and suddenly appeared drained of all the excess nervous energy.

"According to Miss Morgan…"

Shaking his head, Phillip blurted, "Miss Morgan does not know the lengths Julia has gone to, in an effort to help me attempt to secure the hand of another. Her elder sister, in fact. Those are not the actions of a woman in love." He dropped his head and shoulders and remained hunched over in his chair staring at the floor.

"Yet, you were prepared to go to even greater lengths to help your love secure an advantageous match."

Phillip said nothing for several minutes, and his expression was hidden from view. Finally, he swiveled his head and from his crouched position looked up at Caleb. "What should I do?"

Caleb picked a piece of lint from his jacket. "I would think that would be rather obvious. You have already proposed to a woman you do not love. It should be simple to ask a lady you actually *do* love for her hand."

"But I didn't care if Miss Morgan rejected my offer. I think if Julia were to do the same, it would crush me."

"If I had half the assurances you have that I had won Mary's heart, I would be riding as fast as I could and fall at her feet, begging her to have me. I would not even care about the state of my clothes or the fatigue of the ride."

Phillip raised an eye. Caleb was more than a little fastidious when it came to his dress.

The look was ignored, and Caleb added, "You're a fool if you don't act soon."

Julia Looked around the market and saw no signs of

him. She walked to a stall selling vegetables. This location was upwind from the fishmonger. She had never before been to this type of market as she had never been involved in the preparations of her meals. She was grateful Phillip had sent her a cape for her to wear. Without it, her clothes would have caused her to stand out, and she desperately hated being the center of attention. Out of the corner of her eye, she caught sight of two lovely, pastel gowns. She glanced over ever so briefly and saw the women were clearly wealthy and appreciated the attention they were receiving. She was not certain but thought it possible that she had seen one of the ladies at the last event she had attended. She turned back to the tomatoes but as they passed, she caught a small segment of their conversation.

"Do not fear, Miss Morgan's sister is so homely. I am certain that Mr. Weston is only spending time with her in hopes of ingratiating himself with Miss Morgan. And we both know, once he discovers what a cold, heartless woman she is, he will come to his senses."

Julia's heart dropped. It was not that she had any interest in Mr. Weston, but for a heartbeat, she had begun to believe she might be desirable, that she might be worthy of love.

"I had heard rumors that Miss Morgan might be entertaining offers from Mr. Heartford. She did stay by his side for a good portion of the evening."

"I cannot say what the gentleman's intentions are, but I overheard her say that he was a family friend and nothing more."

Julia strained to hear more as the women moved away.

"If he hopes to win her hand, I imagine we can look him up once we are both married and widowed. I am certain he will still be available."

Their voices were now drowned in the sea of noise, and Julia allowed herself to look in their direction. Their retreating backs soon disappeared from sight. Was that how people perceived Allison? Julia felt relief knowing that it was Phillip who was pursuing her. He was loyal and would not be dissuaded by the artificial front her sister presented to the world.

"Julia?"

She spun around to find Phillip. He too wore clothes that permitted him to blend in.

"I am surprised you could find me, Mr. Heartford. I am certain I would not stand out to any of my sister's acquaintances."

"Then your sister's acquaintances are blind," he said. He turned to the owner of the stall and purchased a bag of carrots. After the transaction was concluded, he offered Julia his arm. "I could find you in any crowd," he assured her.

Julia pointed to his bag. "Do your servants not select your produce?"

"They do. But a friend of mine reminded me not long ago about the importance of helping those less fortunate. She made me want to be a better man." He steered them toward a baker and selected several loaves of bread. "I have been buying food each week to send to an orphanage. Sometimes I like to do some of the shopping myself. I can slip in some candies that way."

After he received his bag from the baker, they continued walking between the rows of stalls. Suddenly, Julia stopped. "You saw me with Emma. How did you know? When did you see us?"

His cheeks grew pink. "It is a funny story," he said as a nervous giggle bubbled to the surface. His eyes shifted, and he began to blink rapidly. "As I was returning home, after the first time we met at the barn, I confronted some aggressive shrubbery. This delayed my journey and..."

"I see," Julia said, before he could finish. "You were spying on me." She made the accusation slowly, enunciating each word carefully. She raised an index finger and laid it against her chin. He opened his mouth to speak, but she continued. "In all likelihood, I would have passed you during your scuffle with the greenery. There is no reason why you would not have asked for my assistance. Unless, your accident had been an intentional effort to hide. And those movements you are making with your eyes just now—they leave no doubt."

Phillip bore the expression of a puppy that had been discovered tracking mud into the house. One glance in his direction, and Julia could not help but laugh.

Her merriment appeared to set him at ease, and he said, "That is one of the many reasons I have always liked you. You know me so well."

"And I am rather fond of the fact you are so easy to read," she replied.

"Is that so?" he challenged. His face was wiped of all expression and he stood perfectly still.

She giggled at his antics then looked to the sky. A few fluffy white clouds wearing silver gowns had gathered overhead to watch the pair. Their espial reminded her of the intrusive nature of Phillip's actions. "But why were you watching me?" she asked.

"I was worried about you," he explained. "I wanted to make sure you were not in any danger."

Julia's lips formed a thin line. "I am not a young girl anymore. While I do appreciate your concern, perhaps you should have more faith in my judgment."

Phillip nodded sheepishly. "Will you forgive me if I

give you this?" he said reaching into his pocket. He pulled out a small package wrapped in paper and handed it to her.

"Is this the gift you promised me when we went on the tour of the hothouse?" Julia asked, taking the package gingerly.

"Not a gift. A thank you. It's nothing really. While we were in Kent, I stopped by the confectioner counter and overheard the shopkeeper mention that one of his customers had a particular fondness for the peppermints. I remembered your fondness for them and knew he spoke of you."

Julia felt so touched, her eyes nearly brimmed over with tears. "You remembered?"

"They have been your favorites since you were three."

She put the package in her purse, and cleared her throat, trying to repress her emotions. "Here I am, yet again, wasting your time. We are here to strategize about Allison."

Phillip's confusion was evident. "Allison?"

"Yes, it was clear by the way she chased you off at the park that the probability of you getting her to agree…"

"No," he said hastily. "I no longer intend to pursue that." Phillip looked around. There were people everywhere. "Julia, there is a small park nearby. May I take you there?"

What had he just said? Her heart rate quickened, and she was certain something was wrong. "Whatever for?"

"I need to speak with you, but I would prefer somewhere a little more private."

Julia considered his request for a moment then nodded. The park was very near but, as Phillip had predicted, it was far less crowded. Julia was startled when they reached a somewhat secluded area, and Phillip stopped walking.

He took a step forward, and now, directly in front of Julia, looked into her eyes. "Allison will not have me, and I find she is no longer enough for me." Beads of sweat formed at his temples. "I… that is, my heart has been captured by another."

Julia's apprehension turned into anger. She balled her hands into fists, not caring about the sharp pain caused by her nails digging into her skin. Her teeth ground against each other, but this time she did not stop herself. *How dare he do this to my sister?* "Allison was right; you never stop to think about your actions." She crossed her arms. "A man with such a fickle heart, had no right to speak to our father so soon. You have made a mess."

"The—the desires of my heart have never shifted," Phillip stammered. "I only...that is...I did not...I never loved Allison."

If Julia heard him, she did not show it. "You convinced our father that my sister's time was running out," she stated, with a sharp tone. "You raised his hopes that you would swoop in and save the day." She broke eye contact and shook her head. "You were far too bold when you first approached her. Naturally, she expressed trepidation, and although you swore you would not be discouraged, you have now decided to just give up." Her eyes snapped back up and locked with his. "Have you considered how another lost suitor will impact her reputation? If your heart is so disloyal, why did you wait to give up on her until after making your interest public?"

"My intentions are not public knowledge. I hardly think a private tour on a private estate and speaking to her in public will result in much speculation," Phillip interjected.

"I assure you, your attentions were noticed here. And back home—we are a small community. If you do not think your intentions were obvious to Mr. James, you are a fool. As soon as he says something, word will spread, and speculation will begin."

"That is the second time in this week! Why does everyone keep implying I am a fool?" Phillip mumbled.

Even in her rage, she could hear the irritation in his voice.

"Mr. James will say nothing. He is a good friend and likely has greater respect for your sister for being too wise to accept my offer. But," he continued with a softer, more tender tone, "my heart is not fickle. I would have persisted in my efforts to win her hand, but she helped me see that my heart has always belonged to another."

"Your heart? You, who swore to me that love was unimportant in marriage less than a week ago, now, suddenly find yourself in love?"

"Not suddenly. This love took root long ago, and though I tried to ignore it, block it from sunlight, it has refused to die. I have been in love with *you* for as long as I can remember, Julia." He reached out and touched her arm but the second their skin made contact, she pulled away as if she had been touched by fire.

"Me? How dare you!" Julia's mind raced as she processed what she had heard. "When you discovered my sister would not fall for your charms so easily, you turn to your second choice. Apparently, any Morgan girl will do—even the plain one." She recoiled from him. "You used my own words against me. You concocted some stupid story about discovering your love for me, because I had confided in you. I told you that I believed in love matches." Her eyes filled with tears. "Do you think I am so pathetic I would blindly accept your lies? Is that it?"

"I—wha— No!" Phillip sputtered. He took a step forward, but she held out her arm, immediately stopping him. "I have always loved you. I just had no reason to hope…"

Julia scoffed. "Always loved me? I am to believe that you were in love with me when you asked my sister to marry you? Was it that you loved me, but felt someone pretty might better help you with your political aspirations?"

"Julia, you're beautiful. I have always thought so. I just did not think you could love me."

"And yet it was I who came to you every day asking to see you all those years ago—when you were recovering from your near-death experience. And it was you who refused to speak to me."

"I refused to see you because you had broken my heart, and I was in too much grief from Johnathan's death."

Julia turned from him. "Allison is right. You are a liar. She was smart to refuse you. And while I am sure it is even harder for you to accept, Mr. Heartford, even the homely Morgan girl is unwilling to settle for you." She ran down the path with her hand raised to her mouth leaving behind a broken man.

Chapter Fifteen

Phillip stood with one hand on his hip and used his second hand to emphasize his words. The stance managed to imply superior knowledge on a topic while simultaneously suggesting indifference to it. It was a pose Caleb James had perfected, but it appeared to be an ill-fitting suit on the body of Phillip Heartford. Glaring at Caleb, and using a high-pitched, whiny voice Phillip said, "Just go to her, and tell her how you feel."

Slowly, Caleb shook his head, as if amused. "That is possibly the worst impression of me I have ever seen!" His voice betrayed his indignation.

Ignoring him, Phillip shot back, "Why did I listen to you? You gave me the same stupid advice regarding Miss Morgan." He stomped a few paces away from his host, mumbling to himself, "Always telling me to run off and propose. After five years, you haven't even asked Miss Walker for a courtship!" He spun on his heels and marched toward Caleb. Pointing his index finger, he shook it vigorously at his friend and said, "You are a hypocrite!"

Caleb lifted a strawberry from the tray. "Clearly, things did not go as you had planned, and you are not interested in my suggestions. So, what will you do?" He bit the fleshy part off the strawberry and discarded the stem in a bowl before taking another.

Phillip let out a deep breath, and his body deflated. All of the anger and tension that had been on display moments before, now dissipated, leaving behind a weary, wreck of a man. He walked across the courtyard and pulled out a chair at the table Caleb occupied. Falling into it, he dropped his head and ran his fingers through his hair.

"She won't have me," he said, his voice strained, "and I must marry. The season is not yet over. I guess, I must find someone else." Dark bags hung below his eyes.

Caleb set down the strawberry he'd been holding. "That's it? That is your master plan?"

Phillip turned his head, "I thought we already established I did not require or desire your advice."

"Yes, but that was when we thought you had something better in mind than just giving up."

Phillip stood up. "I appreciate all you have tried to do, but this process is taking too much of a toll. I just want to be done with it." He walked to the low wall that encircled the courtyard and studied the gardens below.

Pouring milk into his tea, Caleb said, "If you feel this is trying, imagine a lifetime with a woman you took because she was the first to say yes."

"I would rather imagine nothing."

Caleb looked up and studied his guest. "You do look as though you could benefit from rest. You should go home and try to think of something else."

"At last you offer sound advice," Phillip said wearily. He soon took his leave.

Upon finding himself alone, Caleb picked up his teacup. He took a sip and then gazed into the distance as he always did when attempting to solve a puzzle.

"You may be able to fool our aunt and uncle, Julia, but

your expressions mirror my own. What is wrong?" Allison pulled back the covers and climbed into bed next to Julia. Once she was comfortably settled, she pulled the duvet up to her chin.

"I don't know what you mean," Julia insisted. She turned onto her back and stared up at the ceiling. "If I seem out of sorts, perhaps, it is because an icicle has just climbed into my bed."

Allison rolled onto her side to face her sister. "This icicle will be placing her cold feet on you if you refuse to confess." Pushing away a strand of hair that had come loose, she added, "I will help you remember." Her tone was firm, a clear indication that she had no intention to let this topic drop. "Given the timing, I assume something happened during your walk this afternoon. Why don't you start there?"

Julia closed her eyes and mumbled, "If you desire a bedtime story, I believe you would find a fairy tale to be more interesting than hearing about my uneventful walk."

"I have already heard all the fairytales you know," Allison assured her. She pushed herself up onto an elbow so she could better see Julia's face. "Tell me, where did you go for your walk?"

After a brief sideways glance, Julia replied, "I went to the bookstore."

Allison grinned. In the darkened room, the light from the candles and fire bounced off the surface of Allison's teeth. "Did that book I ordered arrive?"

"No. I mean, I forgot to ask." As soon as she had said this, Julia winced. The words had come out too fast. She had not sounded convincing.

"You're lying," Allison declared.

Julia could not deny it, but she could attempt to redirect the conversation. "That is a bold accusation," she stated.

Allison's eyes were trained on her sister. "The bookstore has been closed for a week. The owner left town to visit his niece." She leaned in closer and studied Julia as she asked, "Did you go to meet Mr. Heartford?"

Julia's face warmed. She rolled her body away from Allison's so her face could no longer be seen. "No. I did not see him." She could feel her sister's gaze boring into her back. "I went to a different bookstore," she added.

"But I only placed a book order at Marley's, and you know this," Allison informed her. The pillow made a soft crunching noise as Allison lay her head back down upon it. "If you refuse to tell me the truth, Julia, I will need to tell mother about your secret meetings with Mr. Heartford near the barn."

Julia's muscle's tensed, and she remained silent for several minutes.

"I know a great deal about you," Allison taunted. "Have you resumed your secret meetings? Is that where you were? Did he say something that upset you?"

A large grandfather clock stood in the hallway outside their bedroom. Even through the closed doors, the sound of its mechanisms moving filled the space.

"I assure you, you are misinformed." Julia finally said. She had tried to keep her voice even and convincing, but her anxiety had seeped through. "I would never meet with a man without a chaperone. That would be highly improper. But if I had seen Mr. Heartford, I am certain all he would have done would be to confirm as fact each accusation you made against him. I will concede, you were right. He does act without thought, and he is a liar."

Allison shook her sister and demanded, "What did he say?"

"Nothing!" Julia closed her eyes and pulled the covers up to her nose. She knew her sister could not see her face but saw no reason to take chances. "I told you, I have not seen him since our encounter with him at the park." Her muffled voice sounded weary. "But," she added, dropping the covers to ensure her words were clear, "I have reconsidered your position on this matter. I agree that it is not necessary to maintain close relationships with all of our neighbors. If you do not care for Mr. Heartford, I will not push you further to resolve your differences. I imagine you can process your grief for his brother in the best way you see fit."

"I do not dislike Mr. Heartford!" Allison protested.

This declaration was enough to elicit an involuntary response. "Ha! You had me fooled. I have seen you together, and you were very vocal about your disdain for him when we went to the Everlys'."

Outside, a gentle rain began to fall. The droplets hitting the windows provided a soothing patter.

"I was exhausted and tired from being badgered by Papa. Although I do wish he had never asked me to marry him, I was being unfair blaming him for his behavior." The sheets shifted and pulled as Allison twisted the edge in her hands. "You convinced me he is not to blame for the accident. Once I forgave him, I recognized that though he is not the man for me, he is not so terrible. I spoke to Papa before we left. Now that I have promised to look for a match in earnest, Papa is keeping his complaints to a low rumble, which has enabled me to think more rationally." She lifted her hand and bit her nails.

"So, you are ready to consider offers?" Her sister was in no mood to let the conversation drop, but Julia hoped she could steer it into a different direction.

"I am more ready than I was before we had our late-night tete-a-tete. But I really do not have a choice. Apparently, I have only a few months remaining before all hope is lost for me." Allison dropped her hand from her face, and it landed on the bed with a soft thump. "But I am not here to discuss my future. We still have not gotten to the root of your woes."

"I am fine." The words sounded like a moan. "If I do not appear myself, I am sure it is just the stress of the season. I am sure it will pass."

Allison sighed. "I see you are not going to admit this has something to do with Mr. Heartford. I do not blame you. I have been hiding something from you regarding him as well."

Julia's eyes widened and she felt more alert. She turned and faced Allison. The bed shook gently as she shifted.

"I should have told you long ago," Allison continued. She cast her eyes away from the mound of blankets containing her sister. "Sometimes as time passes, revealing that which has been left unsaid becomes harder."

Julia reached out and took Allison's hand. Allison turned back; her brow was wrinkled. "I think keeping my little secret might have caused you pain, but I am trying to make amends." She worried the edge of her lip with her teeth.

"What are you talking about?" Julia asked, her attention now fully focused on Allison.

"Years ago, shortly before the accident, I overheard part of a private conversation between Johnathan and Phillip." Allison withdrew her hands from Julia's grasp and wiped them on the sheets. "Phillip was saying he was very much in love with you but was distraught because he believed he could never earn your love."

Julia shook her head. "Look at me. No man could love me. Not when they see you."

"You do not know how wrong you are." Allison reached under the covers and took back Julia's hand. "You spend your life comparing yourself to me, never seeing that you win. You are beautiful, but you're so much more. You are the one he wants. You are the one he has always wanted."

Julia wanted to roll her eyes. *Is there no end to the things people will say to attempt to convince me of that which I know to be false?* "He wanted nothing to do with me after the accident. That is not how a man in love behaves."

"Maybe not normally," Allison said softly. "But it is how Phillip, who was heartbroken, behaved."

"Is that why you turned down his proposal? Because you believed he once loved me?"

"I…well, I hoped for a love match, and I knew that could never happen with a man who has never stopped loving you…"

Julia released her sister's hand. "No," she barked. "He doesn't love me. What sort of man would ask for your hand if he were in love with me?"

"I have seen the way his face lights up when he looks at you. It is the only time he still looks like the boy we grew up with. I am convinced he will seek your hand. In fact, so is Papa. It is the only reason he has stopped…"

Julia felt sickened at the thought their parents were hoping his attentions would shift. "He's already asked. He knew he had failed with you and saw me as easier prey."

"Julia, you must know that isn't so. I know you saw him today. Did he not tell you of his feelings?"

Sitting up, Julia shook her head. "He just wants a Morgan. He told me what he thought would work. And you just want someone to deflect your unwanted suitor onto."

"I do not!" Allison shouted.

Julia looked to the door, fearing Allison's raised voice could have drawn attention.

In hushed tones, Allison added, "His proposal to me was a sham, Julia! He never once showed me any warmth. His offer was a business arrangement. Please tell me you are not letting his ridiculous, insincere, proposal to me blind you. You cannot possibly be so full of self-pity and pride that you would throw away a lifetime of happiness."

Julia curled back into her ball, facing away from her sister.

"You have always been able to tell when he was lying," Allison continued. "When he spoke of his feelings, could you not see he was being truthful?"

Julia ignored her. The grandfather clock chimed, and with a sigh, Allison rose, took a candle, and crossed to the door. She stood silently, her hand on the doorknob, obviously considering something. "I am going to sleep in the second guest room tonight. You have much to consider."

After the door between the bedchamber was closed, Julia rolled onto her back and stared at the ceiling. She knew she would not find rest that night.

Chapter Sixteen

"Allison?"

She heard her name but tried to ignore it.

"Allison!"

The voice was growing insistent, and she was now being shaken.

Allison's eyes opened just wide enough to see two things. The voice belonged to her sister, and the sun had not yet fully risen. Her eyelashes fell back against her cheek.

"Allison."

"What."

"I need to speak with you. Wake up."

"What time is it?" Allison asked as she stubbornly kept her eyes closed.

"I'm not sure. I didn't look, but just before dawn, I think," Julia said.

"Can this wait?" Allison asked. She rolled on her side and bunched up the covers, hoping they might act as a wall between her and her very loud sister.

Julia ignored the question that had been asked, instead saying, "I thought about what you said...about Phillip...Mr. Heartford. I've made a terrible mistake. I love him, but I said such terrible things."

Allison moaned internally. *Can this wait? Why, yes. It can.* But memories of Julia selflessly comforting her over the years ran through her mind. She summoned enormous will power and sat up. She took her younger sister in her arms.

"Don't worry, poppet. We will fix this. There is an eatery I have wanted to visit, that is rumored to have the best beef pies. We will go there for lunch and will come up with a plan."

Julia pulled away and looked at her sister as if she was talking in a foreign tongue. "Why can't we talk about a plan now?"

"Because you were up all night and you need your sleep. And I think best on a full stomach." Allison stifled a yawn.

Julia frowned.

Allison gave her a stern look. "Given that he proposes at a drop of a hat, I understand your sense of urgency, but I promise, a few hours will not make a difference."

After further urging, Julia returned to her room. Allison sighed and shuffled over to the bell pull. She needed to send Miss James a note.

"Pardon me," Julia said to the man she had just bumped into. She had never been to this establishment. In fact, she had never been to this part of London before, but she could not say she regretted that. The dining area was not particularly small, but it felt minuscule considering the number of patrons that packed the room. Allison reached back and offered her a hand, which Julia took immediately. Though she had never before sailed, Julia imagined falling into the ocean must feel a little like this. She was surrounded by a sea of faces, each as unfamiliar as the next. The movement around her felt like the currents trying to carry her off course. The cacophony of voices, dishes, and footsteps was as intimidating as the sound of waves crashing against each other in a storm. Allison was the beacon of light guiding her to safety, and moments later, they settled into a small table that sat in a corner. Fortunately, the walls remained silent, so Julia's ears were only under assault on two fronts.

Allison shouted across the table. "Considering the popularity of the venue, I imagine the rumor I have heard regarding the pies is true."

"Do they not have any private rooms?" Julia asked.

Allison held her hand to her ear and shook her head.

Julia repeated herself, this time more loudly.

"They are currently full, but we are early," Allison replied.

Julia raised an eyebrow. "Early for what?" she asked.

Whether or not the volume of her voice was sufficient to allow her words to be heard was immaterial. They both knew Allison understood exactly what had been asked, and the expression she bore suggested she also regretted her own words.

"I have heard the crowds thin quickly after one," she replied. "We have arrived a little earlier than I had expected."

Julia was not fully convinced her sister had been forthright in her answer, but it was too difficult to maintain a conversation at the moment, so she instead scanned the room. From the safety of her seat, she could appreciate the allure of the crowd. There was more excitement and energy in this one room than there had been in the entirety of the Everlys' garden party. The crowd was far more varied than she was accustomed to, being comprised primarily of tradesmen and their wives with a few individuals above and below this station.

As Allison had predicted, the crowds began to thin. After placing their order, Julia looked up to find Mr. James entering the establishment. Apparently, Allison had noticed him as well, for she waved him over to their table. Julia's eyes narrowed.

"Mr. James!" Allison exclaimed. "What an incredible coincidence finding you here. Do you come here frequently?"

"Because it is across town, I cannot claim to come here often. But I found myself craving a beef pie this morning. I understand the ones made here are legendary," Caleb confided.

"Yes. I too have wanted to visit since your sister mentioned this place. I was finally able to convince someone to accompany me," Allison replied looking to Julia. "Not ten minutes ago, this place was so full, we could hardly hear ourselves think," Allison said with a smile. "Although it's much quieter now, I see that they still have no tables available. Would you like to join us?"

He frowned and said, "I'm actually meeting a friend."

"I believe our table has enough room for two more, don't you, Julia?"

Julia's mouth went dry. She looked at her sister, wishing she could kick her under the table but knowing it was too late. Not only was it wholly inappropriate to invite a single gentleman to join them, but the purpose of this outing was to discuss a very important matter. She really didn't have a choice about what to say, so she smiled and said, "Of course."

He found the wait staff and added to their order then settled at their table. As Caleb and Allison chatted, Julia wondered if it was possible that Allison was attempting to flirt with Mr. James. But as soon as Phillip Hartford walked through the door, Julia knew exactly what was happening.

"Oh, there he is," Caleb said, as he beckoned Phillip to their corner.

Phillip looked as awkward and uncomfortable as Julia felt, but gracefully took his seat and paid the proper greetings. Even before their pies arrived, both Caleb and Allison had found excuses to leave the table. Allison had claimed she needed to use the privy, while Caleb suddenly remembered he had forgotten to give the groom some instructions for the care of his horse.

Normally, Julia would've been shocked that the gentlemen rode their own horses in town. But given that such transportation provided Mr. James with a reasonable excuse to leave, she understood the purpose.

With the exception of her father, Julia could not recall the last time she had sat alone with a man in public. She felt rather uncomfortable and could not bring herself to look in Phillip's direction. She did, however, have the uncomfortable feeling that she was being watched—no scrutinized—by her dining companion.

A few minutes passed before Julia's eyes swept through the room. Neither Allison nor Mr. James could be found. "Well, Mr. Heartford, I cannot be certain, but I believe Mr. James and Allison have colluded against us."

Amusement danced in his eyes. "Having witnessed Miss Morgan's sister behaving in a similar fashion, I cannot say I am surprised; although, I would argue that they have colluded *for* us."

Julia dropped her head. Her fingers reached up and touched a cross that hung from her neck. "Allison is generally the more mature and seemlier of the Morgan daughters. I am disappointed in her for resorting to such lengths."

Phillip took a sip from his glass and set it down. "I am grateful for it. To be honest, I was not sure what to make of the cryptic note Mr. James sent to me this morning. Now, I believe he must have known how tortured I have been at the prospect of losing your friendship. I think he is attempting to help me."

Julia rolled her eyes. "If that is what they are doing, they are both very rash. Did she even consider what this might do to my reputation? I should not be seen eating with a man without a chaperone."

"You are perfectly safe."

"Of course, I am. We are surrounded by people. But that's not the point." Out of the corner of her eye, Julia saw the waiter approach, carrying their meals. She dropped her chin, hoping to shield her face. Once he was gone, she continued. "Being seen here, alone with you—it will lead to speculation."

Phillip picked up a fork. "I would venture to say, this is a part of London neither of us frequents."

Julia gave him a look hoping to make it clear she did not see the merits of pointing out the obvious.

"Perhaps we are in this establishment because it is filled with no one we are ever likely to again meet." He took a bite of the pie, and his grimace suggested that these pies' reputations were unearned. He set his fork down and pushed the plate away.

She searched the room and was grateful to find he was right—she knew no one. At least she had anonymity.

He cleared his throat and leaned forward. "I have been unable to stop thinking about our last meeting and wish to apologize."

Holding up her hand, Julia replied, "There is no need."

"But there is," Phillip insisted. "Returning to Marymoor, seeing you again, I am reminded of how important your friendship is to me. Almost as soon as I had regained it..." He looked away and took a breath. He mumbled something, and though she could not catch the words, he seemed to be scolding his own inelegance. His eyes lifted and locked with hers. "When we last saw each other, you lectured me on being impulsive and acting too quickly. As soon as you were finished, I professed my feelings. You were right to say I was a fool. Of course, you would be surprised and shocked. I was too forward..."

Julia, who had been studying him carefully, interrupted.

"We have been friends for a very long time, and I will, therefore, speak plainly. While I was angry with you for giving up so easily on Allison, it was not the shock of your declaration that further upset me. I believed your claims to be disingenuous and assumed you were attempting to manipulate me."

"I never lied about my feelings, Julia."

His answer was so swift and certain, Julia's cheeks burned. "But I am so…"

"Perfect?" he suggested. "Beautiful, funny, kind, compassionate?"

Julia took a bite of her food, willing herself not to cry.

"I understand that my feelings are not returned," he continued. "And I acknowledge that I speak of my feelings too freely. But they are genuine, I assure you." His eyes pleaded with her. "But please do not fret that I will expose them again. If friendship is all that you offer me, I will gladly accept.

Julia set down her fork and took a gulp of tea. "I do not believe they were telling us the truth about the legendary pies," she said. After finishing all of the tea remaining in the pot, she added, "It is curious. I have always been able to tell when you speak a falsehood, but I cannot detect any signs of deceit."

"Because I am not being deceitful."

"But you returned for Allison." Tears pooled in the corners of her eyes and she blinked them away. "Why would you do that if you truly loved me?"

Phillip shook his head with a sigh. "It is clear, even now, I cannot hope to gain your love. But I need you to be a part of my life, Julia. I was being greedy. I thought that at the least I could have you as a sister. But that was unfair to Allison and she saw right through me. Please say you will still have me as a friend."

"You honestly came back for me?" Her voice was weak, but it contained a grain of hope.

"Yes," he said. "I refused to admit it at first, but yes. It's always been you."

One of the tears she had been holding back broke free and rolled down her cheek. "I am sorry, Mr. Heartford. I do not think I can accept you as a friend."

His face went ashen. His shoulders slumped forward, and he bore the expression of a crestfallen man.

"To do so would be unfair to your future wife," Julia said. "I would be unable to look at her without feeling a great deal of resentment and envy."

Phillip lifted his chin and looked at her. Confusion, mixed with optimism, played on his features.

"You see, my heart was also claimed long ago," she added. "But unlike you, I have never denied it." She released a long shaky breath. More tears escaped. "When you nearly died, I believed a part of me was lost. When you left, I tried to forget you, to move on, but I couldn't. I could never believe you might feel the same for me, but now..."

His expression became hopeful. "Oh, Julia, I do love you. Are you saying that you..."

Julia finished his sentence. "I am saying that there is a different question you should be asking me, Mr. Heartford."

"Dare I hope you would accept my hand?"

"Not if you do not ask me, Phillip."

He stood and dropped down on both knees. Several of the patrons in the establishment turned and stared. "I will not ask, but I will beg," he said reaching for her hand.

"Get up," Julia hissed. Embarrassment coursed through her veins.

"No. You said that it would be more difficult for a girl to reject an offer if the gentleman's intentions were public knowledge," he explained. His hand encased hers and held it firmly.

"You needn't worry about that... now, get up!" she demanded.

"The Fairy Apprentice would never stand for such insolence," he whispered back.

Julia looked panicked. "Do you not care what becomes of my reputation?" she asked as she attempted to extract her hand.

"Yes," he replied. "Your reputation is of the utmost importance to me, which is why I am here, on my knees. I imagine this display will garner notice when you might have otherwise avoided detection. That might mean to save your reputation, you will need to accept my offer."

"Are you trying to blackmail me?"

"At this point, I am open to whatever works," he said.

Julia lifted a fist to her mouth trying to stifle a laugh. "I will marry you," she whispered, "if you will get up."

Phillip sprang to his feet, and in a loud, clear voice he said, "Miss Julia Morgan, I have waited my entire life to win your hand and you have made me the happiest man in the world by agreeing to be my wife." All of the other patrons now, not only stared at them, but had fallen into complete silence. It was for this reason, they could hear him say, in a far quieter voice, "If you are the prize, I am even willing to come here, eat terrible pies, and make a public spectacle of myself."

"You are thinking of O'Malley's," someone in the crowd shouted. "This place is known for its roast."

Phillip laughed. "Then I would like to order roast all around," he said.

A few of the patrons cheered, and the spell of silence was broken. Phillip sat back in his seat and joined Julia's other hand within his own. "You have not changed your mind?" he asked.

"Within the last two minutes? No, not yet," she teased.

"Not yet?" Phillip loosened his cravat. "In that case, when I bring the contract to your father, I will request a short courtship," he said.

"You have already asked his permission, then?"

"Of course. In fact, he was the one that thought that in a public setting, embarrassment might silence your mind and allow your heart to speak."

"He sanctioned this?" she demanded.

"Only because he knows that we are made for each other, my love."

Chapter Seventeen

Caleb James strode across the field. He had spotted Mr. and Mrs. Heartford and was not going to permit them to leave this year's garden party without saying hello. He ascended the stairs to the terrace only to witness Phillip holding a parfait in one hand and lifting a spoon to his wife's mouth with the other.

"Practicing?" Caleb asked. "I understand if you swirl the spoon around and buzz like a bee, she is more likely to open her mouth."

He glanced down at Mrs. Heartford's abdomen. It would be months before Julia Heartford entered her confinement, but Phillip had shared the news with his closest friends.

"If the baby is a less willing participant, I shall need to try your technique," Phillip replied.

Julia stubbornly turned from the spoon. "Are you suggesting, Phillip, that I eat too freely?"

"Of course not, dear. It is just that now that you are eating for two, I cannot allow you to skip meals. Being the perfect mother, you understand this need."

Julia's mouth opened and she swallowed the bite she had been offered. "I do have a very particular fondness for these parfaits," she said, exchanging a loving glance with her husband.

Phillip returned the spoon to the empty dish. He stepped away, taking these items to a nearby table that held a collection of dirty dishes.

"Well, Mrs. Heartford, are you enjoying life at Marymoor?"

"More than you can imagine, Mr. James. I am blessed that Marymoor is situated so near my parents' home." Julia took a few steps forward and leaned against the railing. "The view from here is simply lovely," she said as she gazed at the gardens below.

Phillip walked up behind her and placed his hand on the small of her back. She gave him a smile that melted his heart.

Turning back to Caleb, she asked, "I have been unable to locate my sister. Have you seen her, Mr. James?"

He reached up and rubbed his chin. "Come to think of it, I have not. And it is rather curious as I felt as though I had scoured the grounds twice searching for the two of you." Caleb looked at Phillip and said, "I had started to wonder if you would simply make another of your ghost appearances."

"Although I would be content to stay with my wife, never leaving the comforts of Marymoor, Julia would not allow it."

Julia raised the edge of her mouth. "You would never achieve your political goals adhering to such a plan."

He reached over and pinched his wife's cheek. "That may have been your initial rationale for attending these functions, but you do not fool me. You have won over the hearts of all of London, and you attend these functions because these are the only times I am willing to share you with your many devotees."

Caleb cleared his throat.

"I apologize Mr. James. I can imagine you find our affection irritating."

"Far from it," Caleb said shaking his head. "When I am fortunate enough to find a wife, I hope she and I will be as blissfully happy as you two appear. However, I did have a second motive for seeking you. I was wondering if either of you has seen Fitz."

"Have you checked the orangery?" Phillip asked.

"You're right. I have scoured the grounds looking for you, but somehow forgot to look in that corner."

"I understand," Phillip said.

"I will never understand your distaste for plants," Julia said to her husband.

"And I will never understand how you thought I could actually prefer your sister," he replied.

They all chuckled, and Caleb bade them farewell.

Julia turned to her husband. "Being here again reminds me of a question I had."

"Should I make a game of it and refuse to answer until you do as I command?"

She smiled up at him and shook her head. "You told me you came to Kent because of Allison. But she had been attending the London season prior to the Everlys' party. Why did you not approach her there?"

Phillip put his hands around his wife's waist and looked into her eyes. "You know the answer to this question."

"Yes, but I never grow tired of hearing it." She smiled coquettishly.

Phillip sighed and eyed her as he might an over indulged child. "I could not admit it to myself at the time, but I came back for you."

A smirk graced her face. "Because you missed your little sister?"

"No," Phillip leaned toward his wife and whispered, "Maybe it was because I missed Uncle Edward who, you will be happy to hear, is on the approach."

Julia's eyes went wide and darted about as if she were a mouse searching for an escape.

Phillip chuckled.

"Do you take pleasure in my predicament, Phillip?" she asked, her panic evident in her tone.

"He is not so bad, my dear."

Uncle Edward was quite a ways away but noticed them and waved frantically. He hurried toward them as fast as his rotund body would carry him. Once he had joined them, he was as red as a beet and out of breath. "Julia," he huffed, "you must come, quickly." He doubled over and took several breaths in quick succession.

"If you are offering tours of the location where you heroically saved a life, Mr. James has not yet had the privilege..."

"No," Edward interrupted, his hand flailing about. His color had started to return to a normal shade and his breathing was more regulated, but it was still a strain for him to speak. "It's Allison," he sputtered.

An icy chill ran down Julia's spine. "Is she hurt?"

Edward shook his head. He stood up, mopped his forehead with a handkerchief, and said, "She has been compromised."

Read More of Cinnamon's Works

The Pathways to Romance Series:
Book #1, To Marry a Morgan
Book #2, The Duke and the Damsel (Release Date June 19)
Book #3, Waiting to Love a Lady (Release Date Summer 2019)

Pride and Prejudice Variations:
Assumptions & Absurdities
Betrothals & Betrayals
Courtship & Corruption
Deception & Debauchery
The Taming of Elizabeth

If you would like to find out more about my books, and when the next release will be available, sign up for my newsletter. I share interesting historical facts and trivia, I think my newsletters are rather funny (but I can't guarantee you'll agree), and I share links to other works by authors who write sweet romances, like me.

I love to catch up with my readers and have both a Facebook Author's Page as well as a Facebook account. You can also e-mail me directly.

I really cannot thank you enough for reading my work. I am always a little shocked, delighted, and afraid when I see a copy of one of my books has been sold. I value all feedback and reviews. Although I do tend to be a little more partial to the positive ones, I really do read all of them and try to embrace all feedback. If you have enjoyed this book, please leave a review and tell your friends. Authors depend on readers like you to help us find an audience for our work.

Author's Notes

Thank you for reading To Marry a Morgan. I started my career as an author by writing stories using Jane Austen's adored characters from Pride and Prejudice. I was very fortunate to stumble into a genre that pays homage to such a brilliant woman. I love books that borrow some of history's favorite heroes and heroines. They allow readers, like me, to spend more time with fictional people that we've already formed attachments to. But, after writing a few such stories, I did want to see if I could create compelling characters of my own.

This series is my first attempt at writing using a world and characters I created. This makes this series a little special for me. There are elements of people I know, and of myself, in several of the characters. In some ways, its freeing to write characters knowing that readers have no preconceived notions about how they might act or behave, but in another way, it is frightening not knowing how they will be received. I guess I will be content knowing that I happen to like this little group of people.

On a separate note, as a writer of historical fiction, I do read quite a lot about the lives and customs of those who lived during and around the Regency Era. I try to be historically accurate. I believe, however, that human nature leads many people to breaking societal rules once or twice in their lives, even in those societies where such rules are considered extremely important. Sometimes, I even allow my characters to do something that was not typically done during that time period. For example, I can imagine that a male character, walking alone on his estate in 1810, might have removed his coat on a sweltering day, even though such an action isn't considered proper by societal standards. I don't feel that putting such an action into a scene makes the story historically inaccurate, but you have the right to disagree. That being said, I am certain I still have an abundance of things left to learn about the period between 1790 and 1880, and I do occasionally make errors. If you are dissatisfied with this, or any of my other stories, because you deem them to be historically inaccurate, I do apologize.

I need to also take a minute to thank a few people who have helped me polish this story and have encouraged me to keep writing even when I doubted myself. This list is probably not comprehensive, but just imagine the music cueing up during the academy awards show and the curtain being pulled across the stage…Thank you, Gianna Thomas, Patricia Holmes, Kay Springsteen, Cheryl Kepler, Meggan Boren, Sandie James, Renee Quinn Yancy, and Melissa Williams-Pope. Thank you, Shaela Kay for designing the cover. And a super big thank you to my readers for your lovely comments, reviews and encouragement. Bill…did I mention my husband Bill?

About the Author

Cinnamon Worth is a San Diego native who is also the youngest of ten children. Growing up, she would listen to her siblings' tales of shenanigans and escapades. Although she did not share her older siblings daring quest for adventure, she did find her imagination offered her all the excitement she craved from the safety of her room.

She discovered a love of reading at a young age and firmly believed that a good book should strive to make the reader feel uplifted. She was later shocked to find that nearly every English teacher she would study under disagreed with this philosophy. After countless hours reading assigned novels that included tragedies, melodramas, and modernism, Cinnamon was eventually convinced to admit that a good book does not require a happy ending. She does, however, strongly advocate for one.

In college, Cinnamon met her Prince Charming and then promptly left him to pursue an opportunity to study abroad in the beautiful English countryside. Fortunately, her Prince was a patient man who waited for her return, and he has since spent nearly 25 years teaching her the meaning of love, showing her the World, helping her to raise two wonderful children, and encouraging her to pursue her dreams.

Cinnamon enjoyed a long career in public sector finance, but she was delighted to leave the corporate world behind in 2014 to focus her efforts on being a homemaker. This shift gave her more time to explore new interests and hobbies which include traveling, cake decorating, crafting, and home renovations. Much to her surprise, she discovered, almost by chance, that she also loved to write.

Hoping to encourage her own children to embrace reading, Cinnamon started writing stories that she thought would cater to their preferences. She focused on plots that centered around popular manga and anime characters. Although she was informed by her children that her stories were, "good but contained too many words," Cinnamon found an audience for her work after posting the stories on the internet. Soon, Cinnamon decided to shift her focus to writing stories based on some of her own favorite characters. Her first five novels have centered on characters from Jane Austin's beloved book *Pride and Prejudice*. The Pathways to Romance Series is the first time Cinnamon is writing using characters she has created. This series, like all of her published work, focuses on romances formed during the Regency Era and relies on emotional, rather than physical, connections to show the progression of relationships.

All of Cinnamon's published works are available on Amazon.com.

The Duke and the Damsel Excerpt

Allison Morgan closed her eyes and leaned her head back. There were dozens of quiet conversations dancing through the air, punctuated by an occasional flourish of a giggle or laugh. If she listened closely, she could hear the soft buzz of bees collecting nectar in the nearby bushes, and the crunch of shoes on the gravel pathways.

The breeze in the trees flickered dappled sunlight through her eyelids. An occasional gust was strong enough to push back the curtains of branches, allowing beams of light to join the party.

Yes, the party at Brighton Manor was again a perfect success. The prestigious guests were well-attired and the food delicious, yet somehow, this year's event was different.

A persistent shadow alerted Allison that someone stood beside her. When she opened her eyes, they landed on Miss Trimble.

The older woman frowned. "Are you well, Miss Morgan?" she asked. She reached out her hand. It was covered in a dingy glove clearly so worn it should have been retired.

With effort Allison refrained from jerking away.

"Why don't you let me get you some food?" Miss Trimble asked, motioning to one of the many tables filled with desserts. "One of the best things about being on the shelf is that we no longer need to worry over our figures."

Had this been said to bolster Allison's mood, it had failed miserably. "I will be perfectly fine. I think I am simply restless. Will you excuse me?"

Miss Trimble nodded, and Allison left the shade provided by the cluster of oaks. As of late, she was finding she preferred the company of plants. They never talked or cast looks of pity in her direction. When she had decided to accept a life of solitude, she had not understood just how much humiliation would accompany it. Still, shame was a small price to pay for self-protection.

The path leading toward the hothouse was lined with bushes that had been perfectly clipped into a long, lush green wall. As Allison walked, her hand to trailed along the tips of the tiny leaves. She hadn't gone but a few yards when she felt something brush against her neck. She reached up to find the small gold chain, that held her cross, missing. She retraced her steps, her eyes peering at the ground. Soon she spotted the gold as it glittered in the light. She had just bent down to collect her necklace when she heard her name spoken on the other side of the manicured hedges.

"Did you see Miss Morgan standing near Miss Trimble?"

"Yes. Isn't it sad? If I were her, I wouldn't get too close. One wouldn't want to be thought of as an old maid by association."

Laughter filled the air.

Allison caught her breath. She may have feared that this was how others thought of her, but hearing it confirmed was far worse.

"It did make me wonder, if she has not yet found a match, how will I manage?"

"Miss Morgan may be pretty, Gertrude, but I have heard her heart is as cold as stone. She is incapable of warmth much less love."

"I do not know how to pretend to be in love. Must I act in such a manner to elicit an offer?" The anxiety in Gertrude's voice was clear.

"No. Just be sure to at least be friendly. If you need to be reminded how not to behave, spend some time with Miss Morgan."

Allison waited for the peals of laughter and footsteps to grow faint. She rose from her crouched position and wiped a tear from her cheek before returning her jewelry to her neck. Opening her reticule, she found a handkerchief and blew her nose. *If my heart bears a resemblance to stone, then I have successfully protected it. I do not care what they say. I am safest alone.*

Her pace quickened. She knew being surrounded by plants would lighten her heart, and she needed such refuge more than ever.

The door to the greenhouse swung open, and Fitz Atherton's head began to pound. Remaining seated he folded, then set down his news sheets. He looked toward the doors, and there, gliding toward him, was Caleb James. "How did you find me?" he snapped.

"Well, hello to you as well, Fitz," Caleb replied. He joined his friend at the small tea table. "I see you are in a fine mood. Since you have chosen to remain on the grounds of Brighton Manor this year, I take it you are enjoying the garden party."

Fitz picked up his reading materials, unfolded them with a loud, if not vigorous shake, and replied, "I didn't have a choice. My father forbade the coachmen from taking me anywhere without him by my side." He scanned the left page of the newspaper, and finding nothing of interest, asked, "You never said how you found me."

"Phillip actually. I feel as though I've found two unicorns today. It is rather extraordinary to have you both stay through the social portion of the weekend." Caleb began drumming his fingers on the table, causing Fitz to drop the corner of his paper and give him a stern glare.

"Stop that. You are causing vibrations."

"Yes. I am aware," Caleb replied. He did not stop the drumming but rather began tapping the table as well, using his second hand. The effect was a rhythmic pattern that wasn't entirely unpleasant.

"Are you attempting to be extra annoying, or have I simply been away from you for so long I have forgotten your normal obnoxious state?" He again folded his paper and set it aside. "I should have known Phillip would send you to me."

"Because he is a generous man, willing to share me with the world?"

Fitz uncrossed his legs and leaned into the table. "No. He has wanted to get even with me for a very long time because I told you where he hides the key to the drawer that holds his finest cigars."

"Ah. He does have excellent taste." Caleb stilled his hands. He reclined, throwing one arm over the back of his chair and allowing his legs to lay stretched out in front of him. He looked very much like a rag doll that had been dropped onto the chair. "Well, now that I have your attention, I must say, I am a tad hurt by the reception. Since when did you find me so distasteful?"

Fitz eyed his friend suspiciously. "Aren't you here to drag me back to my father, so I can meet another charming and talented lady?"

"I am not. But," he said, reaching out and taking a lump of sugar from the bowl sitting on the table, "is your aversion to the charm or the talent?"

"The monotony. They are all the same." Fitz picked up his teacup and took a sip. He returned it to its saucer and said, "They are only interested in robbing me of my freedom."

"I hardly think the women are to blame. Your father appears to be the one most intent on you marrying." Caleb popped the sugar into his mouth. "Do you think you will be able to ignore him indefinitely?"

"Well, since his health isn't what it once was, indefinitely could be less time than you imagine." Fitz lifted a cookie from the plate and took a bite. "So yes, I think I can wait him out. I just need to continue to be subtle in my efforts to ensure I am rejected. At least from those prospects he knows of. It is far less effort to rid myself of those women attempting a direct assault without his knowledge."

"It is times like these I am reminded of my good fortune to not be born to a titled father." Caleb sat up. "Incidentally, what happened to Brown?"

"Who?" Fitz's eyebrows squeezed together in confusion.

"Brown. The spare bachelor? Isn't he the one you carry around in your pocket to throw out as the sacrifice these days?" Caleb took a cookie from the tray and tried to spin it as one would a toy top. The cookie must have lacked symmetry, for it floundered and fell over almost instantly.

Understanding, Fitz jerked up his chin. "Oh, him. He announced his engagement last week. He is dead to me." It was clear from his tone that his words were not without jest.

Caleb smiled. "I take it he did not marry the lady in pursuit of you."

"He did not. And, to make matters worse, that same vulture is here today. She is after me with a vengeance."

Slowly nodding, Caleb asked, "Which one is she again? They change so frequently…"

"No. Of course. You cannot be expected to remember them all when I can barely do so myself." He took another sip. "It was Miss Allen. She was speaking to that fellow you introduced me to, DeVoss."

"Evan DeVoss?" Caleb's eyes went wide. "If she was speaking to him you needn't worry. Her affections should have already shifted. That man is as charming as..."

"The day is long?" Fitz offered.

"Ah. Very good. Shakespeare. But no. I was going to say as me."

Fitz rolled his eyes.

"Come now, you must own I possess some virtues."

"You do, but charm is not a virtue. I would prefer honesty any day."

"Then you would not care for DeVoss." Caleb pushed an errant lock of his hair back into place. "He is full of charm but duplicitous. During that awkward time when I did not understand how to demonstrate to the world my many attributes and likability, he mentored me, actually. I am grateful he taught me. Yet, I cannot claim him as a friend. But you can consider your Miss Allen problem solved."

Fitz nodded his approval. "Well, I am glad to hear it. Miss Allen is nothing if not persistent."

Fitz reached into his pocket and retrieved his watch. A glance confirmed he had at least another hour before his father would be prepared to leave the party.

"You haven't found a replacement?" Caleb asked.

This drew Fitz from his thoughts. "What?"

"For Mr. Brown."

"Oh. Yes, I have. But he came down with a fever last night. He sent word first thing in the morning. That is why I must hide away here. I appreciate DeVoss's assistance with Miss Allen but without some protection, I wouldn't dream of exposing myself in this setting." Fitz took another sip of his tea.

Caleb nodded. "Well, the reason I've come to find you is that there is a young chap asking after you. Maybe you can enlist his help fending off the throngs of maidens willing to marry you for money and title." A raised eyebrow from Fitz seemed to cause Caleb to divulge more. "I am not sure of his purpose, but he goes by the name Alsworth."

Fitz's mouth fell to the floor. For a moment he thought he may have misheard. "Alsworth was able to secure an invitation to your aunt's party? That is appalling!"

"He was not invited directly," Caleb explained. Caleb pulled on the cuffs of his shirt until a half inch of each sleeve peered out from his jacket. "He came as a guest of one of my uncle's friends Mr. Walkon. Walkon is a little daft and does not always show good judgment in selecting his friends. Since I'd never heard of this Alsworth, I thought I should find out if he is your friend or foe so that I might direct him toward or away from you."

"And what direction applies to each?" Fitz asked. Caleb shot him a look and Fitz continued. "The man is not quite either, actually. He owes me money. More than he can afford. I imagine he is hoping to arrange an agreement."

"So, do you want to be found?"

Fitz paused, considering the question. "Not particularly," he said at last. "But the man is a bit of a weasel and has abhorrent manners. It is probably better I see him here, away from anyone important. I would rather not be associated with him, and one never knows what sort of scene he might make."

Caleb stood. "Very well. I will send him to you."

Caleb had nearly reached the door when Fitz called out, "If you are returning to the party, could you also have some tea sent to me? I am nearly out."

With a lopsided smile, Caleb bowed in a dramatic fashion. "Of course, my lord. I am but your humble servant."

Once Caleb was gone, Fitz looked at the cookie that his friend had tried to spin. *I should have asked him to send a replacement.* He picked it up, set it on the plate, and pushed the plate away. After recovering his papers, he flipped through it until he'd found an article of interest. Quickly, he became absorbed in his reading and lost track of time. Not until the door to the room swung open and the sound of the footfall reached his ears, did he realize he was no longer alone. Knowing those were the footsteps of a woman, he reasoned that it must be the maid.

"You can set it down here," he said without dropping his paper.

"Oh, I apologize, sir. I had no idea anyone would be in here."

What on earth could she be talking about? Why would she bring tea to an empty conservatory?

Fitz bent down the corner of his paper and glanced in the direction of the voice. To his great shock, there stood a woman who was most certainly not a maid. It took him a moment to collect his thoughts. *Why would a well-bred woman leave a party to wander in the bowels of Brighton Manor alone?* Suddenly, the answer became very clear.

"Miss, if your aim is to try to trap me, you must be cleverer than that."

She stuck out her jaw and anger flashed across her eyes. "Pardon me?"

"I say, you will find no husband here. So, hurry on back to the party where you might have more luck."

"What!" Allison's face grew red. "I would not marry you if every other man on earth dropped dead. You are no gentleman, sir!"

"And I have made no claims to the contrary. Now go away."

Her eyes flickered toward the door.

Fitz was satisfied. She would be going now.

But then she crossed her arms and raised her chin. "I don't think I will," she declared, looking down her nose at him.

Fitz glared at her. "You do understand the damage that might be done to your reputation should you be discovered here, alone with an unmarried gentleman, do you not?"

"I thought you did not claim to be a gentleman."

"Right. All the more reason to flee."

She glanced nervously at the door again.

He could practically feel her anxiety. He was close to convincing her. He just needed to make it very clear that even though they had never met, he knew her. He had met dozens of girls exactly like her, and no matter how good she was, he could not be fooled. "I can see you want to do the right thing. Now, do not view retreat as a failure. You tried your best. Consider this practice for someone a little less seasoned. I, unfortunately, know your type far too well, I'm afraid."

Her head snapped back into place. "My type?" Her eyes narrowed in on him "What exactly do you mean—my type?"

"Oh, the pretty maiden who dreams of wealth and started her first season with hopes of marrying the most sought-after bachelor." He stood up and took a few steps forward to get a better look. He allowed himself to assess her. His eyes roamed over her carefully. "I am sure you nearly succeeded. But the gentleman's parents swooped in to save him. With your prince gone, there was a line of offers out your door, but none were quite worthy enough." He began to circle around her. She was beautiful. He would give her that. "When you returned the next season, you still had suitors, but they were actually inferior to the last batch. You assumed it was just that year's crop—never suspecting rumors about you were circulating." As he continued to move around her, he drew closer. He could see he was making her nervous, and that was what he wanted. If she feared him, she would go. "Now, a little long in the tooth, you have grown more desperate. You are not yet willing to take one of those nobodies, but the son of a Duke is worth your while, even if he comes with a bit of a reputation."

Allison's mouth hung open in disbelief, and her eyes had grown large. He took two more steps toward her and was now so close he could feel her shallow breathing. They were watching each other, each feeling like prey but attempting to be intimidating. The sound of the door opening startled Fitz. When he turned toward the entrance, there stood Alsworth. Fitz knew he was in trouble.

52025119R00094

Made in the USA
Middletown, DE
06 July 2019